Three-Minute Tales

Stories from Around the World to Tell or Read When Time Is Short

Margaret Read MacDonald

August House Publishers, Inc.
ATLANTA

For my stepmother, Jane Stone Veal Read,
who always has a funny tale to tell us over the supper table.

—MRM

Published 2004 by August House Publishers, Inc.

www.augusthouse.com

Printed in the United States of America

| 10 | 9 | 8 | 7 | 6 | 5 | 4 | 3 | 2 | 1 | HB |
| 10 | 9 | 8 | 7 | 6 | 5 | 4 | 3 | | | PB |

LIBRARY OF CONGRESS CATALOGING-IN-PUBLICATION DATA

MacDonald, Margaret Read, 1940–
    Three-minute tales : stories from around the world to
tell or read when time is short / Margaret Read MacDonald.
       p.   cm.
    Includes bibliographical references.
    ISBN-13: 978-0-87483-728-5 (cloth)
    ISBN-13: 978-0-87483-729-2 (paper)
    1. Tales. 2. Short story. I. Title.
    GR74.M33   2004
    398.2—dc22   2004046257

The paper used in this publication meets the minimum requirements
of the American National Standard for Information Sciences—
Permanence of Paper for Printed Library Materials, ANSI Z39.48.

CONTENTS

ABOUT THIS BOOK

In this collection I try to provide a sampling of short tales for many uses—tales for those who work with the young and for those who tell to adults. I have tried to find a balance between some of my favorite short stories, which are probably already known to many tellers, and a selection of unusual tales that most will not have encountered before. I also gave myself permission to include a few tales I have already published elsewhere, since these were some of my very favorite short short tales.

Since I could only include around eighty stories here, I have included bibliographies to lead you to more of my favorite short tales. I hope these will help you build for yourself a fine repertoire of tiny tales for telling.

My editor thought it would be useful for me to note the time it takes to tell each of the tales. So I got myself a stopwatch and went to it. I tried to tell at a moderate pace, but the truth is that my speech is rapid no matter how hard I try to slow myself down. After clocking one of these tales at 2½ minutes, I decided to read it again, this time in the slow drawl of storyteller Joe Hayes (Joe had just visited our library system so his rhythms were still in my head). Telling the same story at this pace took 4 minutes, 15 seconds. So you may want to factor in your own speaking pace when referring to these clock times.

ABOUT THE TALE NOTES

In the notes I give reference to the following folktale motif-indexes, which have cited these stories:

Aarne, Antti and Stith Thompson. *The Types of the Folktale.* Helsinki: Folklore Fellows Communication, 1961.

Baughman, Ernest W. *Type and Motif Index of the Folktales of England and North America.* The Hague: Mouton, 1966.

MacDonald, Margaret Read. *The Storyteller's Sourcebook: A Subject, Title, and Motif-Index to Folklore Collections for Children.* 1st edition. Detroit: Neal-Schuman/Gale Research, 1982.

MacDonald, Margaret Read and Brian W. Sturm. *The Storyteller's Sourcebook: A Subject, Title, and Motif-Index to Folklore Collections for Children: 1983–1999.* Farmington Hills, Michigan: Gale Group, 2000.

Thompson, Stith. *Motif-Index of Folk-Literature.* 6 vols. Bloomington: Indiana University Press, 1966.

My intent is to demonstrate that these stories are told in other variants elsewhere in the world.

WHY THREE-MINUTE TALES?

It is always a good idea to have a few very short stories in your pocket when you set out on the storytelling trail. They are easy to tell and easy to teach to children or adults.

Their brevity also makes them easy to *remember*; therefore, you always have a few tales that you can tell at the drop of a hat. They are great fillers for those unexpected wee time slots when you are left with fifty kids to manage while their teacher runs off on an emergency mission ... or when you have whizzed through your nicely planned program and are approaching the end with five minutes to go on the auditorium clock.

Here are some further uses for these short tales:

Beginning storytellers: easy-to-learn first tales.

Repertoire boosters: a quick and easy way to add a wider variety of cultural and topical material to your repertoire.

Classroom teachers: Short tales for that unexpected found moment in your day. These are easy to tell, or if you prefer, fun to just read aloud.

School visits: It is indeed useful to have a few short stories up your sleeve to pull out when your program doesn't go exactly as expected. Somehow, you end up with three minutes left before the bell—just enough time for a very tiny tale!

Museum tours: Docents have to move groups of children through the galleries in a timely fashion, yet they like to share stories to enhance enjoyment of the objects in the collection. Very short stories are vital to these transitions. In Chapter 2, I've included some tales I shaped for use in Asian collections.

History walks: Local history walks work best too with very short tales. One useful technique is to break longer stories into briefer segments so that only a bit is told at each stop.

Nature Walks: Naturalists or Scout leaders on nature walks like to share a few short stories as they go. Time is short, and the audience is usually on their feet, so the three-minute story is perfect.

Speakers: Speakers are always on the lookout for very short tales to liven up a talk and involve the audience. Nothing focuses an audience and draws them to the speaker like a story.

Media appearances: Radio and TV interviewers often ask if you have a short story to tell. Of course, thirty seconds would please them most, but some of the one-minute tales included here may suit the need.

Teaching tool for storytelling classes: These short stories make excellent first stories for beginning storytellers. I spread out copies of stories such as these, let the students select one each, and give them five minutes to read it over. Then I instruct the students to go and stand facing a wall of the classroom. When I give the signal to start, each student is to begin telling the story out loud to the wall. They are to work on projection and gestures as they tell. After about ten minutes, I call them back to their seats and each student stands up and tells the new story to the class. I do this on the very first class session so that the students have already had a successful storytelling experience before they leave class. George Shannon's riddle-tale collections (see Bibliography on pages 159–160) work very well for this. I usually do one session with riddle tales and later in the course another session using wisdom tales.

So browse through the book. Find some tales that you really like. And add them to your bag of tricks.

SUGGESTIONS FOR THE BEGINNING TELLER

This book contains short, simple stories that you should be able to make your own without much work. Do not try to memorize these. Simply share them in your own words. Feel free to adapt the stories to fit your own style, your own persona. Each story changes as it passes from person to person. The tales have simply been frozen in text here for a moment. As soon as you lift the story off the page, it comes to life and begins to change again. That is the nature of the folktale tradition. Pick up a tale and join in!

Here are some suggestions for preparing these tales for performance:

SELECT:

Select a story you want to tell. This is a story you would like to share with others.

READ:

Read the story aloud. Listen to the sound of the words; feel the meanings.

Read the story aloud again. Consider how you want to interpret the words with your voice and your body.

TELL:

Stand up and use your entire body to tell the story you have just read. Check back with the text if you forgot something, but keep telling to the end of the story.

Tell it again. Project your voice as if you were speaking to a room full of listeners. Try to get all the way through without checking your text this time.

Tell it again. Imagine your audience in front of you. Project; use your body. Enjoy the tale!

REHEARSE:

Review the story in your mind as you go about your daily routines for a few days. Tell it to yourself as you take a walk. Tell it out loud to yourself in the shower.

PERFORM:

Find an audience and tell the story!
Tell it again and again and again!

The story is now in your body. You can tell it in the future, whether you are standing or sitting, with broad gestures or none at all. Your body has internalized the story through this learning technique.

Tales to Tell
on a Walk

It can be useful to have a pocketful of stories to share when out for a walk with children. Because the stories given here are rather fanciful, they may be less useful for those giving nature walks. But for the family going on a stroll, they are perfect. For many more such stories, see Anne Pellowski's *Hidden Stories in Plants: Unusual and Easy-to-Tell Stories from Around the World, Together with Creative Things to Do with Them* (New York: Macmillan, 1990). Also check the excellent sources cited in her bibliography.

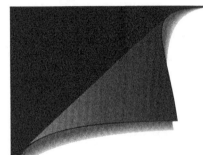

The Sun Sisters

A Chinese Legend

1 minute

Long ago, two maidens lived on the moon.
The sisters spent all of their days embroidering.
They had seventy-two embroidery needles!
Oh, how skillfully they used them.

People would stare up in the evenings and wonder at the maidens' beauty.

"Look at the beautiful maidens on the moon!"
"Aren't they lovely?"
"See how delicately they embroider?"

The maidens were very embarrassed by this.
They had no privacy at all.

One day they called to their brother, who lived in the sun.

"Brother, would you change homes with us?
People are always staring at us.
We don't like living here."

"But at night there are few people about.
If you lived on the sun,
many people would see you during the daytime."

"Oh no, they won't. We have a plan."

So the brother changed places with the sisters.
You can see the man in the moon is still there.

As for the sisters, you can never see them.
For if anyone dares to look toward the sun . . .
they stick their needles in his eyes!

And such pain is caused by the seventy-two embroidery needles of these maidens
that no one ever looks directly at the sun.

Retold from "The Modest Sisters" in *Picture Tales from the Chinese* by Berta Metzger (Philadelphia: J.B. Lippincott, 1934), pp. 78-80. MacDonald's *Storyteller's Sourcebook* classifies this as Motif A736.1.1.1★ *Sun sisters and moon brother.* She cites one Chinese version in Francis Carpenter's *Tales of a Chinese Grandmother* (Garden City, New York: Doubleday, 1937). This story can be told when warning children of the dangers of staring directly at the sun.

The Butterfly Robe
A Chinese Folktale

1 minute, 35 seconds

The prime minister of China was exhausted with court life.
People were often scheming and grabbing to advance their own cause.
He needed to escape for a while.

So, still dressed in his radiantly beautiful court robes, he climbed into his
sedan chair and asked his bearers to carry him up into the hills.

There he got down from his chair and strolled away over the meadow.
The flowers were so beautiful.
He sat down on a stone and reveled in the beauty around him.

Sitting thus, so still . . .
he saw a bee fly from a flower and land on his bright robe.
"Oh! You think my robe is a flower, don't you?
Well, here . . . you may have a bit."
And drawing his sword, he cut off a snippet of the fabric and tossed it onto
the green grass. "Here, bee! A flower for you!"

Then, laughing, he cut off another piece of the bright fabic.
"Here, bees!
Take it if you like it!"
And he tossed this piece high into the air.

The piece of silk floated through the air and landed lightly on an open
flower.
Then . . . it rose and began to flutter from flower to flower.

"What is this?"
He cut off another piece and flung it after the first.

And this piece too began to float about the field,
fluttering beautiful silken wings.

More and more pieces he flung into the air.
And soon the field was shimmering with the beautiful creatures.

The prime minister stopped.
He was wearing nothing but the ragged remains of his robe.

But the field was alive with . . . butterflies.

The prime minister set off for his home a happy man.
The tormenting life of the court awaited him,
but he was revived now.
He had created something of beauty.
The wonder of that would sustain him the rest of his life.

Retold from *Picture Tales from the Chinese* by Berta
Metzger (Philadelphia: J.B. Lippincott, 1934), pp. 99–
102. Motif A2041 *Creation of butterfly*. In his collection
Black Folktales (New York: Richard Baron, 1969),
Julius Lester includes a tale in which God creates but-
terflies by snipping off bits of flowers.

Planting Forget-me-nots
A Folk Legend from Iran

■ 1 minute, 20 seconds

An old tale tells of a heavenly creature who fell in love with a daughter of the earth.

When first he caught sight of her,
she was sitting by the river edge, decorating her hair with forget-me-nots.
How beautiful she was!
He spent every day sitting by her side on the river's bank.
He would pick forget-me-nots for her
and watch in rapture as she wove them into her hair.

And then he was discovered.
When it was found that he had been consorting with a human,
he was banned from paradise.

That is, he was barred from paradise until . . .
his love had planted forget-me-nots in every corner of the world!

For love of him, she undertook this task.
For years the girl wandered the earth,
planting forget-me-nots wherever she went.

At last her task was finished.
In every corner of the earth tiny blue forget-me-nots could be seen to bloom.

She was no longer a young girl, but still her heavenly lover stayed faithful.

When they returned to the gates of heaven to report that the task was done,
the heavenly gates opened . . . not just for him . . . but for her as well.

"Your love is greater than your wish for life," said the keeper of the gate. "Because you know the meaning of truly unselfish love, you may enter heaven without death."

To this day forget-me-nots bloom wild in many places throughout the world.
Their sight reminds us of the importance of love.

Retold from *Myths and Legends of Flowers, Trees, Fruits and Plants in All Ages and in All Climes* by Charles M. Skinner (Philadelphia: J.B. Lippincott, 1911), p. 119. For another tale of the origin of forget-me-nots see "Forget-me-not" in *Celebrate the World: Twenty Tellable Folktales for Multicultural Festivals* by Margaret Read MacDonald (New York: H.W. Wilson, 1994), pp. 83-87.

Tales to Tell on a Museum Tour

Telling a few stories during a museum tour enhances appreciation of the objects being viewed. The listener remembers the story—and with it, the exhibit. The story can provide information about the object in a gentle, non-didactic way. Brevity is important here, though. There is a full tour to complete, and the children have a short attention span because of the excitement of the objects yet to be seen and the activity of other museum visitors passing by. When I plan stories to teach for docent use, I first tour the museum looking for objects that I know have fine stories. It is also important that there be a place to perch a classroom of students near the cases where the docents will be telling the stories.

The tales given here were shaped for use by the Asian Museum in San Francisco and for the Burke Museum in Seattle. I shaped three different segments of the Buddha's life story so that each could be told in front of a different museum piece. In most museums housing Asian art you will find several representations of the Buddha, and there is often an image of the naga sheltering a seated Buddha. Any exhibit of Chinese art or culture will likely have a depiction of a dragon somewhere, sometimes on a piece of clothing.

Keep these tips in mind when selecting stories for a museum tour:

- Tour the museum and make note of striking art objects.

- Make note of the spaces in the museum in which a group of children could sit down to listen to a story. Note which objects are near enough for the children to gaze on while you tell.

- Check your library, the Internet, friends, and museum guidebooks to identify stories related to the objects you find most interesting.

- Bring with you to the museum a list of the stories from that cultural area which you already have in your repertoire. Look carefully for possible connections. If you can connect some of the stories you already know to the exhibit, you will save yourself a lot of legwork!

- Imagine yourself as a child sitting before an exhibit. How can you shape your story to make it most accessible to this child? Which stories does this child need to hear?

Siddhartha Encounters Suffering

A Tale from the Buddhist Tradition

▊▊▊▪ 2 minutes, 45 seconds

In all of his life, Prince Siddhartha had seen nothing but beauty and happiness. He had three palaces—one for the cold season, one for the hot season, and one for the rainy season. The prince spent his entire life within palaces. He grew up, married, and had a son. Still he knew nothing of the real world.

One day Siddhartha heard the women singing of beautiful forests beyond the city. This was something he *had* to see. He made plans for an outing to the Padmasanda Grove.

When the king heard of this, he sent word that every old or sick person should be hidden away from the route the prince would take. Only the young and beautiful should be allowed along that route.

So when the prince rode out in his golden chariot, the streets were lined with beautiful people. The roads were strewn with purple lotus blossoms, the city bright with flowers.
How happy Prince Siddhartha felt to be prince of this beautiful kingdom.

But suddenly, an old man stepped in front of his chariot. He was bent and frail.
Even with a cane he could hardly walk.

"Stop the chariot!
What sort of man is this? I have never seen such a feeble creature."

His chariot driver replied, "Why, this is old age.
All men become like this in the end."

"You mean *I* will become like this?"

"Yes, of course. In time."

"How can I go on a picnic when such things exist in the world?
Back to the palace!"

The charioteer whirled the golden chariot around and they raced back to
the palace.

Sometime later, the prince thought again that an excursion to the grove
might be fun.
Again the king sent out word to remove all old and ill people from his route.
Again the streets were strewn with flowers and lined with beautiful young
people.
The prince smiled as he drove through the streets in his golden chariot.
But then . . .

A very sick man staggered in front of the chariot.

"Stop the chariot!
What sort of person is *this*?
His body is covered with sores.
He can hardly stand."

"This is a man racked by disease," said the chariot driver.
"It is a misfortune that falls on many."

"You mean other men also have such disease?"

"Yes, many men suffer this."

"Back to the palace!"
The chariot driver whirled the golden chariot about and sped back to the
palace.

Yet once more the prince decided to visit the forest grove.
Once more the king sent word for the way to be strewn with flowers and
lined with smiling young people.
But just as the prince was happily passing . . .

Four men stepped in front of his chariot . . . carrying a corpse.

"Stop the chariot!
What is *that*?"

"That is a dead man.
He no longer lives and breathes.
His body is being taken away."

"Does this happen to other men too?"

"Yes. It happens to all men. Even you one day will die."

"I cannot go play in the grove when such things are possible," said the
prince sadly.
"Back to the palace."

But the chariot driver did not obey.
The king had told him to take Prince Siddhartha on to the pleasure grove,
regardless of his commands.

And there the prince sat under the beautiful trees
with nothing but sadness in his heart.

Retold from *Asvghosa's The Buddhacarita or Acts of the
Buddha* by E.H. Johnston (Delhi: Motilal Banarsidass,
1936). A wonderful retelling of this material appears
in *The Hungry Tigress: Buddhist Legends and Jataka Tales*
by Rafe Martin (Berkeley: Parallax Press, 1990).

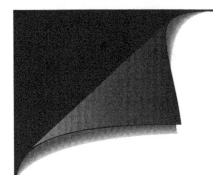

Siddhartha
Under the Bo Tree
A Tale from the Buddhist Tradition

 1 minute, 30 seconds

After his encounters with old age, disease, and death, Prince Siddhartha vowed to renounce his princely world and become a monk. He left the palace and entered the forest to live simply and meditate.

Siddhartha thought he could attain enlightenment by starving his body. At first he ate only one bowl of rice a day. Then half a bowl. Then a quarter bowl. Finally he was taking only one grain of rice each day as food.

He was very close to death. Then he remembered something. When he was only a small child he had once had a moment of clarity and great understanding. If he could come so close to enlightenment then as a well-clothed and well-fed baby, perhaps starvation was not the way.

He decided to eat again. At that very moment a young maiden from the village came to him, offering milk-rice for his bowl. Siddhartha accepted the offering and ate.

Then weakly he made his way to the edge of the river. "If this is the day of my Supreme Enlightenment," he pronounced, "may the bowl float upstream." And he threw his bowl into the water.

Immediately the bowl began to whirl upstream . . . until it reached the whirlpool of Kala Naga Raja, The Black Snake King. And there it was sucked down, down . . . and landed with a *clink* beside a row of identical bowls in the Naga King's jeweled palace.

Now Prince Siddhartha knew that his enlightenment could be attained. So he seated himself on a heap of freshly cut grass at the foot of a bo tree and began once more to meditate.

Retold from these sources: *The Hungry Tigress: Buddhist Legends and Jataka Tales* by Rafe Martin (Berkeley: Parallax Press, 1990) and *Asvghosa's The Buddhacarita or Acts of the Budddha* by E.H. Johnston (Delhi: Motilal Banarsidass, 1936). The many bowls in the palace of Kala Naga Raja remind us that many had sought and attained enlightenment before Siddhartha. Kala Naga Raja is not the same naga as Mucalinda, who sheltered the Buddha during his meditation and is depicted often in art.

The Naga Mucalinda Shelters the Buddha

A Tale from the Buddhist Tradition

■ 1 minute, 10 seconds

When the Buddha attained enlightenment he continued to meditate for seven weeks.
During the second week he stood and gazed at the beautiful bo tree under which he was sitting when he received enlightenment.
But during the sixth week he sat by the side of a nearby lake.
While he was deep in meditation, a storm came up.
Heavy rains fell, and cold winds blew around him.

Seeing this, Mucalinda, a great naga, came from his dwelling and coiled his body seven times around the Buddha's body to keep him warm. Then it spread its hood over Buddha's head to protect him from the rain. The storm lasted for seven days. And when the rain stopped, the naga uncoiled itself, took the form of a young man, and bowed to the Buddha.

Then the Buddha spoke, saying:

Happy are those who are content
and those who have learned The Way and truly see.
Happy are those who have good will
toward all living creatures.

Happy are those who have no attachments
and those who have no desires.
But the disappearance of the word "I AM"
Is the greatest happiness.

Retold from *Asvghosa's The Buddhacarita or Acts of the Buddha* by E.H. Johnston (Delhi: Motilal Banarsidass, 1936).

A Lover of Dragons
A Chinese Tale

■ 35 seconds

Zighao, the Lord of Yeh, was so fond of dragons that he had them carved
and painted all over the house.
There were beautiful dragons on his chests,
glowing dragons on his walls,
magnificent dragons on his doors.

He let everyone know of his great love for dragons.

The dragon in heaven, hearing of this,
flew right down to earth.
He poked his huge head into Zighao's door
and swung his tail through the window.

Zighao ran screaming out the back door and away as fast as he could.

This shows that Zighao was not truly fond of dragons.
He just like what looked like a dragon . . .
not the real thing.

Retold from "The Lord Who Loved Dragons" in
Selected Fables, edited by Yue Yin Wuen (Beijing: New
World Publishing, 2002), pp. 4–5. This is related to
Motif W.121.1 *Hunter wants to be shown lion tracks, not
lion himself.* Stith Thompson cites European variants
and Aesop. In a related Aesop cited by MacDonald,
dogs tear up a lion skin, fear living lion.

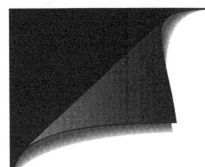

Ganesha
Around the World
A Legend from India

1 minute, 30 seconds

Ganesha was a sweet child . . .
even though he had the head of an elephant . . .
and a fat, fat little body.
His mother, Parvati, adored him.

One day Ganesha and his brother, Shanmukha, were fighting over a peach.
Their parents, Shiva and Parvati were annoyed with the boys.
Their father, Shiva, said:

"Why don't we solve this with a contest?
You two boys can race around the world.
Whoever gets back first may have the peach."

The brothers thought this was a great idea.
Shanmukha climbed onto his steed, which was a magnificent peacock.
Ganesha climbed upon his steed . . . which was a tiny mouse!

Mythology is strange sometimes . . . but that's the way it was!

Parvati watched her sons and smiled.
Shiva gave the signal to. . . . *Start!*

Shanmukha flew off on his peacock, raising a cloud of dust and disappear-
ing in an instant. Off he was on his amazingly fast flight around the world.

Ganesha looked at up at his parents and smiled.
Then he slowly rode his little mouse around his parents seven times.
Then he bowed to them and put out his hand for the peach.

"What? Ganesha, you haven't even begun your journey yet!" laughed Parvati.

But Ganesha bowed again.

"Mother and Father, *you* are the whole world.
You are the mother and father of the universe."

This was true.

"And you are the whole world to me.
I just walked around you.
Thus I have walked around the whole world."

Parvati and Shiva laughed.

"Son you are wise.
Yes, the peach is yours."

And when a bedraggled Shanmukha came flying in,
he had to laugh too, at the wisdom of his brother.
Anyway, he had lost the argument
but just had a really great flight around the world!

Retold from *The Broken Tusk: Stories of the Hindu
God Ganesha* by Uma Krishnaswami (North Haven,
Connecticut: Linnet Books, 1996), pp. 7-11. This source
uses the name Muruga for Ganesha's brother. Other sources
name him Shanmukha and set the fight over a bride. It is
said that Ganesha then married the two beautiful daughters
of Vishwabrahma, Siddhi and Buddhi. For more versions see
www.freeindia.org/biographies/gods/ganesha/page9.htm.

Tales for the Youngest Listeners

Very young children can actually enjoy quite lengthy stories if the tales are well chosen and engagingly told. However, here are a few three-minute tales for those days when you want to insert a quick tale. Note that some of these stories work equally well with older children and adults. Never relegate a story exclusively to a preschool repertoire.

Coyote's Rain Song

A Navajo Tale

1 minute, 30 seconds

Coyote stood on the hill overlooking prairie dog town.
Coyote thought.

"I am hungry for prairie dog meat.
I'll make it *rain*.
I'll make it rain on prairie dog town.
I'll wash those prairie dogs
right out of their holes!"

Coyote began to chant his magic rain-making song.

Rain! Dark Cloud, Rain Cloud!
Rain on prairie dog town!
Rain! Dark Cloud, Rain Cloud!
Rain on prairie dog town!

Rain! Rain! Rain!Rain!

Coyote chanted his song four times.
Four is the magic number.

SECOND CHANT:

Rain! Dark Cloud, Rain Cloud!
Rain on prairie dog town!
Rain! Dark Cloud, Rain Cloud!
Rain on prairie dog town!

Rain! Rain! Rain! Rain!

THIRD CHANT:

Rain! Dark Cloud, Rain Cloud!
Rain on prairie dog town!

Rain! Dark Cloud, Rain Cloud!
Rain on prairie dog town!

Rain! Rain! Rain! Rain!

FOURTH TIME IS THE *MAGIC* TIME:
Rain! Dark Cloud, Rain Cloud!
Rain on prairie dog town!
Rain! Dark Cloud, Rain Cloud!
Rain on prairie dog town!

Rain! Rain! Rain! Rain!

It began to rain.

It rained to the *north* of prairie dog town.
It rained to the *south* of prairie dog town.
It rained to the *east* of prairie dog town.
It rained to the *west* of prairie dog town.

But it did not rain
on prairie dog town.

The prairie dogs laughed at Coyote
Slinking away in the rain.

"Your song is no *good*, Coyote . . .
Your song is no *good* . . . ."

Retold from "Coyote's Rain Song" in *Twenty Tellable Tales: Audience Participation Folktales for the Beginning Storyteller* by Margaret Read MacDonald (New York: H. W. Wilson, 1986), pp. 20-23. The story was retold from Natalia Belting's *Our Fathers Had Powerful Songs* (New York: Dutton, 1974). She cites the tale as Apache, but all other variants I have seen are Navajo. The notion of Coyote singing down the elements seems to appear in several Navajo tales, for example "Navajo Folk Tales" in *Journal of American Folk-Lore XXXVI*, pp. 371-372 and "Navajo Texts" by Edward Sapir and Harry Hojier, pp. 20-25. For more sources see MacDonald's notes in *Twenty Tellable Tales*.

Pancake Party
A Siberian Folktale

1 minute, 30 seconds

Little Mouse, Raven, and Snow Ptarmigan lived together in a cozy
little tent on the tundra.
They cooperated very well...most of the time.

One morning Little Mouse woke up thinking of pancakes.
"Let's make pancakes today."
"I love pancakes!" said Raven.
"Me too!" said Ptarmigan.

"Who will go to town to buy the flour?"
"Not me," said Raven. "I'm too busy."
"Not me," said Ptarmigan. "I'm busy, too."

"Then I'll go myself," said Little Mouse.

And she did.

Little Mouse pulled her sled down to the store.
She bought the flour.
She pulled her sled back home again.

"Here is the flour.
Now who will mix the batter?"

"Not me," said Raven. "I'm still busy."
"Not me," said Ptarmigan. "I'm still busy, too."

"Then I'll mix it myself," said Little Mouse.

And she did.

Little Mouse put in flour.
She put in egg.

She put in water.
She stirred that batter until it was smooth.

"The batter is ready.
Now who will fry the pancakes?"

"Not me," said Raven. "I'm still busy."
"Not me," said Ptarmigan. "I told you I was busy."

"Then I'll fry them myself," said Little Mouse.

So she did.

Little Mouse made her griddle very hot.
She poured batter on her griddle.
She flipped the pancakes over and fried them on both sides.
Soon she had a pile of pancakes all ready to eat.

"The pancakes are ready.
Now who will eat the pancakes?"
"I will!" said Raven.
"I will!" said Ptarmigan.

"Oh no, you won't." said Little Mouse.
"You watched while I went for the flour.
You watched while I mixed the batter.
You watched while I fried the pancakes.
So you can watch while I eat them!"

And they did.

She sat right down and ate those pancakes up...every one.

And since the pancakes are finished...well, so is this story.

From *Kutkha the Raven: Animal Stories of the North*
translated by Fainna Solasko (Moscow: Malysh
Publishers, 1981). Motif W111 *Laziness*. MacDonald
W111.6★ *The little red hen and the grain of wheat.*
Versions cited there are British, one Irish.

Hiring the Fox as Shepherd
A Folktale from Norway

1 minute, 35 seconds

An old woman needed someone to watch over her sheep when they were out in the fields.

The bear volunteered for the job.

"Well, I don't know.
You seem very gruff.
How would you call my sheep if you were their shepherd?"

"I would call them like this ...
Grouff! Grouff! Grouff!"

"Oh, no no no!
That would frighten my sheep.
They would all run away!
I do not want you to be my shepherd."

The wolf applied for the job.

"You seem rather snarly.
How would you call my sheep, if you were their shepherd?"

"I would call them like this ...
"Waooooo! Waooooo! Waooooo!"

"Oh, no no no!
That would scare my sheep to death!
They would all run away!
I do not want you to be my shepherd."

Next came the fox to apply.

"Well, you seem like a respectable fellow.
How would you call my sheep, if you were their shepherd?"

"I will call very gently,
and the sheep will all come right to me.
I will call like this . . .
Little sheep . . . little sheep . . .
It's time to sleep!
Gili-bome . . . gili-bome . . .
Come home . . . come home!"

"Oh, how sweet!" said the old woman.
"You are just the one to take care of my sheep.
You can be my shepherd."

So the fox took the sheep out to the fields next day.
And when he brought them back . . .
The old woman did not notice that one was missing.

And the next day . . .
And the next day . . .

On the fifth day, the old woman suddenly noticed that
Where she once had had ten sheep . . .
She now had only five!

And looking closely, she saw sheep's wool and blood on the fox's muzzle.

"So, that's how it is!" she thought.
And picking up her heavy churn full of milk, she heaved it at the fox.
"You are fired!"

"Ow! Ow! Ow! Ow!" the fox ran off.

But since that day many foxes have white spots on the end of their tails.
That is where the old woman splashed him with her churn full of milk.

And of course everyone knows . . .
If you want your sheep to come home safely . . .
Do not hire a fox for a shepherd!

Retold from "The Fox as Shepherd" in *Valery
Carrick's Tales of Wise and Foolish Animals* by Valery
Carrick (New York: Dover, 1969), pp. 1-8 (first pub-
lished by Frederick A. Stokes in 1928). Also in Peter
Asbjørnsen and Jørgen Moe, *Norwegian Folktales*
(New York: Viking, 1960), pp. 106-107. Motif K934
*Fox as shepherd. A woman in search of a shepherd tried the
voices of applicants. The wolf, the bear are rejected, the fox
accepted.* MacDonald cites Norwegian variants. Type
37 *Fox as Shepherd.* Aarne-Thompson cite Latvian and
Norwegian variants. Also Motif A2215.5 *Fox struck
with churn dash: hence white tail.* Stith Thompson cites
Finnish and Estonian variants.

The Frog from Osaka and the Frog from Kyoto

A Folktale from Japan

1 minute, 45 seconds

A frog who lived in Osaka once decided to travel to Kyoto.
He had heard that Kyoto was a marvelous city,
and he was eager to see it.

Meanwhile, a frog from Kyoto decided to travel to Osaka.
He had heard that Osaka was a fantastic city.
He was eager to visit there.

It took these tiny frogs a long time to climb the mountain road.
For days each kept up their struggle,
higher and higher on the mountain road they climbed.

It happened that the two frogs met right at the top of the mountain.
How amazed they were to see each other!

"I am going to Kyoto!" said the frog from Osaka.
"I've heard it is marvelous!"

"I am going to Osaka!" responded the Kyoto frog.
"I've heard the same thing about Osaka!"

"It's too bad we aren't taller," said the Osaka frog.
"If we were just a bit taller we could look ahead at our destinations.
This has been such a hard journey.
I hope it is worth it."

"But I have an idea!" said the Kyoto frog.
"Why don't we hold onto each other and stand up on our hind legs?

Then we could each see the city that lies ahead."

"What a great idea!"

The two frogs grasped each other around the shoulders.
Each stood wobbling as tall as possible on its hind legs
facing toward the city it hoped to visit.

"What!" exclaimed the Kyoto frog.
"Osaka looks just like Kyoto!"

"Imagine!" said the Osaka frog.
"Kyoto looks exactly like Osaka!"

"It's a good thing we checked this out.
We might as well save ourselves the long trip and go back home."

So the two bid each other farewell and each started hop . . . hop . . .
hopping back down the mountain.

They had forgotten just one thing.
The frogs' eyes were at the back of their heads.
Thus the Kyoto frog was really staring back at the city he had just left.
And the Osaka frog was staring at his hometown.

Still each frog lived out his days happily,
content in the knowledge that the other city was just like his own!

Versions appear in *Violet Fairy Tales* by Andrew Lang
(New York: Longmans, Green, 1901), pp. 111–113.
Motif B296.2★ *Two traveling frogs meet at mountain top.*
Standing up to look at other side of mountain decide desti-
nation is identical to home so they return home. They had
forgotten that their eyes are in back of the head, so each
looked back the way he had come.

Participation Tales

The stories in this section are the sort often used at camp. They will probably already be familiar to the experienced teller, but I wanted to include them here for the beginners who will use this book. I include also a few story-songs as these too can be useful when filling a short time spot. Note that most of these tales and songs can be expanded to take much longer, if that is your need.

The Teeny Tiny Man
A Canadian Finger Play

 2 minutes

Here's a teeny tiny man	Hold up **right** thumb.
in a teeny tiny house.	Wrap right fingers around right thumb.
Here's a teeny tiny man	Hold up **left** thumb.
in a teeny tiny house.	Wrap left fingers around left thumb.

And they play all day at hide and seek.
A teeny tiny man through his window peeps.

Right thumb peeps between fingers.

If no one is looking, he softly creeps
out of his door. He comes so slow.　　　Right thumb crawls out of fist.

Looks up and down.
Looks high and low.　　　Right thumb looks up and down.

Then back into his house he goes.　　　Right thumb tucks back into right fist.

This teeny tiny man through his window peeps.

Left thumb peeps between fingers.

If no one is coming, he softly creeps　　　Left thumb comes slowly out.
out of his door. He comes so slow.

Looks up and down.　　　Left thumb looks up and down.
Looks high and low.

Then back into his house he goes.　　　Left thumb tucks back into left fist.

Sometimes the teeny men forget to peep.　　　Both thumbs come out.
Out of their doors they softly creep.

Look up and down. Look high and low.	Both thumbs look up and down.
See each other and laugh: "Ho! Ho!"	Turn thumbs to face each other, make them jump.
Then back into their houses they go.	Tuck thumbs back into fists.

Adapted from *I'm a Little Teapot! Presenting Preschool Storytime* by Jane Cobb (Vancouver: Black Sheep Press, 1996), p. 92. "Mr. Brown and Mr. Black," another version of this finger play, can be found in *Stories to Play With: Kids' Tales Told with Puppets, Paper, Toys, and Imagination* by Hiroko Fujita (Little Rock: August House, 1999). The story is often told as "Mr. Wiggle and Mr. Waggle." A web search will bring up several variants. The storyteller Papa Joe has a particularly well-developed one on his website at www.pjtss.net.

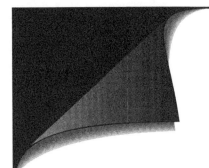

Two Goats on a Bridge
Reshaped from Eastern European and Russian Folklore

 2 minutes

VERSION #1

A Western Hill.

Hold up right fist; encourage audience to participate.

An Eastern Hill.

Hold up left fist.

A small bridge between.

Point to an imaginary bridge.

A goat lived on the Western Hill.

Hold up right index finger.

A goat lived on the Eastern Hill.

Hold up left index finger.

Sometimes the goat on the Western Hill would go down,
cross the bridge, and eat grass on the Eastern Hill.

Right finger goes down, crosses imaginary bridge, nibbles, and returns.

Sometimes the goat on the Eastern Hill would go down,
cross the bridge, and eat grass on the Western Hill.

Left finger goes down, crosses imaginary bridge, nibbles, and returns.

One day both goats tried to cross the bridge at the same time.

Both fingers come to bridge.

"Back off!" said the goat from the Western Hill.
"I was here first!"

"Back off yourself!" said the goat from the Eastern Hill.
"It is *my* bridge."

The two pushed and shoved.	Fingers push and shove until …
And as neither would give way, they eventually pushed each other off of the bridge.	Fingers fall … … *splash!*
As the wet goats trudged away, They could be heard to mutter, "Wasn't *he* an uncooperative fellow!"	Two fingers face away from each other and leave.

VERSION #2

A Western Hill.	Hold up right fist; encourage audience to participate.
An Eastern Hill.	Hold up left fist.
A small bridge between.	Point to imaginary bridge.
A goat lived on the Western Hill.	Hold up right index finger.
A goat lived on the Eastern Hill.	Hold up left index finger.
Sometimes the goat on the Western Hill would go down, cross the bridge, and eat grass on the Eastern Hill.	Right finger goes down, crosses imaginary bridge, nibbles, and returns.
Sometimes the goat on the Eastern Hill would go down, cross the bridge, and eat grass on the Western Hill.	Left finger goes down, crosses imaginary bridge, nibbles, and returns.
One day both goats tried to cross the bridge at the same time.	Both fingers come to bridge.
"What? This bridge is too narrow!" said the goat from the Western Hill.	Fingers wiggle as goats talk.

"We have a problem!" said the goat from the Eastern Hill.

"What can we do?"

"Let's see . . . "

"Maybe if we both squeezed carefully . . . .
we could pass each other."   Squeeze two fingers past each other.

And the two goats squeezed carefully past each other and went on their
way to eat grass.

As they munched away, they could both be heard to mutter,
"Wasn't *he* a cooperative fellow!"   Fingers nod at each other.

One question:
Which kind of goat are you?

Retold from "Two Goats on the Bridge" (a Russian
folktale) and "Two Goats on the Bridge" (an Eastern
European folktale) from *Peace Tales: World Folktales to
Talk About* by Margaret Read MacDonald (North
Haven, Connecticut: Linnet Books, 1992), pp. 5-6,
53-54. This book was published in Indonesia as
Cerita-Cerita Pelestarian Lingkungan (Yogyakarta:
Penerbit Kanesius, 2003). While touring Indonesia, I
needed an even easier version to use in workshops for
orphanage caregivers and young Earth Kids volun-
teers. In desperation I came up with this finger-play
approach. It was easy for the translators to handle. And
the workshop participants all "got it" right away.

That's Good!
No, That's Bad!

An American Folktale

▌ 1 minute

> Instruct audience to say "That's good!" or "That's bad!" after each statement. Teller can hold up right hand for "That's good!" and left hand for "That's bad!" if the audience needs cues.

TELLER:	AUDIENCE:
A boy went for a ride in an airplane.	That's good!
No . . . that's bad. The airplane engine failed.	That's BAD!
No . . . that's good. The boy had a parachute.	That's good!
No . . . that's bad. The parachute didn't open.	That's BAD!
No . . . that's good. There was a haystack under the boy.	That's good!
No . . . that's bad. There was a pitchfork in the haystack!	That's BAD!
No . . . that's good. He missed the pitchfork.	That's Good!
No . . . that's bad. He also missed the haystack.	

> Signal with eyes, hands, and body language that this finishes this silly
> story. The result should be groans from the audience.

Retold from "Good or Bad" in *I Saw a Rocket Walk a Mile* by
Carl Withers (New York: Holt, 1965), p. 22, and the picture
book *Fortunately* by Remy Charlip, illus. by author (New York:
Maxwell MacMillan International, 1993). Motif Z51 *Chains
involving contradictions or extremes.* Type 2014. *MacDonald Z51.2★
The airplane crashed. Haystack there, missed the haystack, etc.* See
also the Norwegian tale cited in MacDonald as Motif Z51.3★
*Hare tells fox of his marriage. Good. No, that's bad. A real devil. Bad.
dowry and house—good—house burned down. Bad—she with it.*
MacDonald also cites a Slovenian variant which is set up as a
"'that's a lie" tale. Motif Z51.4 *Task: making girl's mother say
"that's a lie." (H342.1). Harvested nine tubs of cabbage. That's good.
Rotted. That's bad. Oak trees from compost. Good. Hollow. Bad. Full
of honey. Good. Bear ate. That's bad. Squeezed nine tubs of honey
from bear. "That's a lie!" Weds girl.* MacDonald/Sturm cite a
British variant of the "house is burnt down . . . wife in house
story." Motif Z51.1 *The house is burnt down.* Type 2014A *The
House is burned down.—That is too bad.—That is not bad at all,
wife burned it down.—That is good.—That is not good, etc.* Aarne-
Thompson give Estonian and Rumanian variants. Compare
this tale also to "Bad Luck or Good Luck?" on
page 136 of this collection. Professor Emeritus Spencer Shaw
of the University of Washington does an inimitable version of
this little story. His body language as he tells this tale takes it
well beyond the text. On paper it doesn't look half so good!
Have fun trying to breath life into it.

Did You Feed My Cow?
A U.S. Folk Chant

▌1 minute, exluding time needed to teach
audience cues and responses

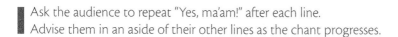

▌Ask the audience to repeat "Yes, ma'am!" after each line.
▌Advise them in an aside of their other lines as the chant progresses.

LEADER	AUDIENCE
Did you feed my cow?	Yes, ma'am.
Will you tell me how?	Yes, ma'am.
What did you feed her?	Oats and hay.
What did you feed her?	Oats and hay.
Did you milk my cow?	Yes, ma'am.
Will you show me how?	Yes, ma'am.
How did you milk her?	*Swish. Swish. Swish.*
How did you milk her?	*Swish. Swish. Swish.*
Did my cow die?	Yes, ma'am.
Did my cow die?	Yes, ma'am.
How did she die?	*"Unh! Unh! Unh!"* (holding stomach)
How did she die?	*"Unh! Unh! Unh!"* (holding stomach)
Did the buzzards come	Yes, ma'am.
For to pick her bones?	Yes, ma'am.
How did they come?	*Flop! Flop! Flop!*
How did they come?	*Flop! Flop! Flop!*

My favorite version of this folk chant is that used by
Professor Emeritus Spencer Shaw of the University
of Washington. My version is based on his. A written
version is found in *Did You Feed My Cow? Street
Games, Chants, and Rhymes* by Margaret Taylor
Burroughs (Chicago: Follett, 1969).

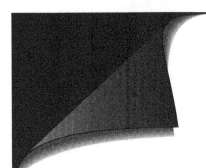

The Tailor's Jacket
A Jewish Folktale

⏸ 2 minutes, 15 seconds

A poor tailor was once given a bolt of cloth by a rich customer.
"You must use this for yourself," said the customer.
"You deserve a fine coat for the winter."

The tailor was overjoyed.
He set to work at once.

He measured and he cut,   Mime measuring and cutting; encourage
                                            audience to join in.

he measured and he cut.
He sewed and he sewed,   Mime sewing, encourage audience to join in.
he sewed and he sewed . . .
and he made himself a fine new coat!

How the tailor loved that coat!
He wore that coat..
He wore that coat . . .
He wore that coat . . .
until the coat was all worn out.

The tailor could see that, even though it was worn in places,
there was still enough material to . . .
make a jacket!

So he measured and he cut.
He measured and he cut.
He sewed and he sewed.
He sewed and he sewed . . .
and he made a jacket!

52

The tailor was proud of his new jacket.
He wore that jacket everywhere.
He wore that jacket . . .
He wore that jacket . . .
He wore that jacket . . .
until it was all worn out.

The tailor looked at the ragged jacket.
He could see that, even though it was worn in places,
there was still enough material to . . .
make a vest!

So he measured and he cut.
He measured and he cut.
He sewed and he sewed.
He sewed and he sewed . . .
and he made a vest!

The tailor was proud of his new vest.
He wore that vest everywhere.
He wore that vest . . .
He wore that vest . . .
He wore that vest . . .
until it was all worn out.

The tailor turned the vest this way and that.
He could see that, even though it was worn in places,
There was still enough material to . . .
make a cap!

The tailor loved that cap!
He wore that cap everywhere.
He wore that cap . . .
He wore that cap . . .
He wore that cap . . .
until the cap was all worn out.

The tailor turned that cap around and around.
When he looked closely, he could see that,

even though it was worn in places,
there was still just enough material left . . .
to make a button!

So he measured and he cut.
He measured and he cut.
He sewed and he sewed.
He sewed and he sewed . . .
and he made a button!

The tailor was proud of that button.
He wore that button everywhere.
He wore that button . . .
He wore that button . . .
He wore that button . . .
until the button was all worn out.

The tailor was just about to throw the button away.
But he looked at it closely and saw . . .
there was just enough material there . . .
to make a STORY.

Retold from "The Tailor's Jacket" in *Earth Care: World
Folktales to Talk About* by Margaret Read MacDonald
(North Haven, Connecticut: Linnet Books, 1999),
pp. 94-96. This story is beloved by many storytellers.
It is short and makes a great intro or exit from a
storytelling session. It can be told with audience par-
ticipation, if you wish. Let the audience chant with
you and make appropriate motions on the lines "He
measured and he cut," "He sewed and he sewed," etc.
(This story also works beautifully *without* audience
participation. Let your setting decide.) For a singing
version of the story, see Doug Lipman's audiotape *Tell
It With Me* (Albany, New York: A Gentle Wind, 1985).
This is Motif J1115.4. *Clever tailor.* MacDonald/Sturm
J1115.4.1★ *Tailor makes vest from worn out coat.* See
MacDonald/Sturm and *Earth Care* for more variants.
My version is influenced by many tellers, most espe-
cially Nancy Schimmel and Robert Rubinstein.

Herman the Worm

American Camplore

Back where I used to live there was a little worm that came by the house real regular.

His name was Herman.

And that little feller could actually talk.

Don't know how he came by that.

None of the other worms around there ever spoke to me.

But Herman would come by nearly every evening and chat a bit.

We'd all be sitting out on the front porch, and here Herman would come.

We'd tell him about the news with our family.

And he'd tell about the news with his family.

He had a brother and a sister still at home with his mother and father.

And he used to talk about them a lot.

In those days Herman was ... oh ... about this big.

> Show small size with hands.

But one day Herman came by and ... he was THIS big.

> Show bigger size.

"Why, Herman! What happened to you?"

"Well," he says, "it's like this.
I ate my brother."

"You ate your brother! That's a terrible thing to do!"

"Hey! I'm a *worm.*"

And Herman crawled off.

Next day here he came again.
Only now he was THIS big.   Show larger size with hands spread out.

"Herman, what on earth?"

"I ate my sister."

"What a *terrible* thing to do!"

"Hey! I'm a *worm*."

Next day here he came, and now he was THIS big!
                                   Show bigger size with hands.

"Herman! No!"

"I ate my father."

And the next day, you can imagine . . . .
Herman was THIS BIG!   Show size with hands spread far apart.

"Not your mother, too!"

"I ate my mother."

Now Herman was so huge that he could hardly crawl back home.
I didn't think I'd ever see that worm again.
But don't you know the very next day here he came.
And he was this big.   Show small size.

"Herman, what happened?"

"Well, it's like this.
My whole family got to churning around inside me
And they churned and they churned until . . .
I burped."

And he settled down on the porch to tell me all about his mother and
father and brother and sister and how they were getting along back home.

The Girl scouts and other campers tell it like this:

Sittin' on my fencepost, chewing my bubblegum
Chew.. chew . . . chew . . .
Playin' with my yoyo . . . *weee . . . oo! weee . . . oo!*
When along came Herman the Worm.
And he was this big.
And I said, "Herman? What happened?"
"I ate my sister."

Sittin' on my fencepost, chewing my bubblegum
Chew.. chew . . . chew . . .
Playin' with my yoyo . . . *weee . . . oo! weee . . . oo!*
When along came Herman the Worm.
And he was this big.
And I said, "Herman? What happened?"
"I ate my brother."

Sittin' on my fencepost, chewing my bubblegum
Chew.. chew . . . chew . . .
Playin' with my yoyo . . . *weee...oo! weee . . . oo!*
When along came Herman the Worm.
And he was this big.
And I said, "Herman? What happened?"
"I ate my mother."

Sittin' on my fencepost, chewing my bubblegum
Chew.. chew . . . chew . . .
Playin' with my yoyo . . . *weee . . . oo! weee . . . oo!*
When along came Herman the Worm.
And he was this big.
And I said, "Herman? What happened?"
"I ate my father."

Sittin' on my fencepost, chewing my bubblegum
Chew.. chew . . . chew . . .

Playin' with my yoyo . . . *weee . . . oo! weee . . . oo!*
When along came Herman the Worm.
And he was this big.
And I said, "Herman? What happened?"
"I burped."

I heard this story many years ago. Several tellers were
telling it, and I thought it was a cute little tale. I told it
a couple of times myself and then forgot about it.
Recently, Herman came back. But now he is a camp
chant! I have no idea if Herman began as a tale and
became retold as a chant, or if he started as a chant
and was retold as a narrative. But here are both versions. You can take your pick. The chant form allows
for lots of audience participation. Of course, in both
versions you show the ever-increasing worm size by
measuring with your hands.

Under the Spreading Chestnut Tree

An American Camp Song

1 minute, if sung through once

 Make five motions in succession (see below).

Under the spreading chestnut tree,
under the spreading chestnut tree,
we're as happy as can be,
under the spreading chestnut tree.

Under	Hands held flat above head.
Spreading	Arms stretched wide.
Chest	Thump chest.
Nut	Knock on head.
Tree	Hold arms high as waving branches.

I learned this simple camp song long ago at the Methodist Camp Riverside in southern Indiana. A slightly different version appears in Virginia Tashjian's *With a Deep Sea Smile* (New York: Little Brown, 1972), p. 122. It is fun to repeat this omitting one word at a time. Sing "Under the spreading chestnut ____". Then "Under the spreading chest ___ ____." Continue until the entire song is done only in the motions.

Lazy John
An American Folksong

2 to 3 minutes, depending on the
number of items you buy for Lazy John

Lazy John, Lazy John . . . will you marry me?
Lazy John, Lazy John . . . will you marry me?

How can I marry you
with no shirt to wear?

Up she jumped and away she ran,
down to the market square.
There she bought a hat
for Lazy John to wear.

Lazy John, Lazy John . . . will you marry me?
Lazy John, Lazy John . . . will you marry me?

How can I marry you
with no pants to wear?

Up she jumped and away she ran,
down to the market square.
There she bought some pants
for Lazy John to wear.

This continues as John asks for socks, shoes, a hat, etc.

Lazy John, Lazy John, *now* will you marry me?

How can I marry you?
With a wife and ten children at home!

I learned this American folksong from North Carolina storyteller Jim Wolf while on tour
in Northeast Thailand. Virginia Tashjian includes the song in her *With a Deep Sea Smile*
(Boston: Little, Brown, 1974). She suggests using the song as a boy–girl call-and-response
song. This can be done easily if the teller simply cues the boys for their next line.

Roll Over

An American Folksong

■▌▌■ 2 minutes, 30 seconds, or longer if
acting it out with live, rolling bodies!

▌ Roll hands on "roll over" lines.

There were ten in the bed, and the little one said,
"Roll over! Roll over!"
So they all rolled over and one fell out.

There were nine in the bed, and the little one said,
"Roll over! Roll over!"
So they all rolled over and one fell out.

There were eight in the bed, and the little one said,
"Roll over! Roll over!"
So they all rolled over and one fell out.

There were seven . . .
Six . . .
Five . . .
Four . . .
Three . . .
Two . . .

There was one in the bed, and the little one said,
"It's all MINE!"   Stretch arms and legs wide.

A good version of this well-known children's song appears in *I'm a Little Teapot! Presenting Preschool Storytime* by Jane Cobb (Vancouver: Black Sheep Press, 1996), p. 64. In a preschool setting, it is fun to bring in a blanket and act this out. This can also be done as a finger play. Hold up ten fingers to start. Drop one for each verse. On "roll over" the children roll their hands around each other.

The Courting Song

An American Folksong

1 minute, 30 seconds, but can be expanded by creating more tasks for Old Woman

Teach the audience to sing the "SPEAK a little louder sir!" lines before you begin. They should place a hand behind one ear and lean forward as they holler this line.

LEADER:

Old Woman, Old Woman,
Are you fond of spinning?

Old Woman, Old Woman,
Are you fond of spinning?

AUDIENCE AND LEADER:

SPEAK a little louder, sir!
I'm rather hard of hearing.

SPEAK a little louder, sir!
I'm rather hard of hearing.

LEADER:

Old Woman, Old Woman,
Are you fond of carding?

Old Woman, Old Woman,
Are you fond of carding?

AUDIENCE AND LEADER:

SPEAK a little louder, sir!
I'm rather hard of hearing.

SPEAK a little louder, sir!
I'm rather hard of hearing.

LEADER:

Old Woman, Old Woman,
Are you fond of courting?

Old Woman, Old Woman,
Are you fond of courting?

AUDIENCE AND LEADER:

SPEAK a little louder, sir!
I'm just beginning to hear you.

SPEAK a little louder, sir!
I'm just beginning to hear you.

LEADER:

Old Woman, Old Woman,
Will you let me marry you?

Old Woman, Old Woman,
Will you let me marry you?

AUDIENCE AND LEADER:

Lord have mercy on my soul!   Throw hands in air in amazement.
I think that now I hear you!

Lord have mercy on my soul!
I think that now I hear you!

We sang this song over and over when I was a Girl
Scout back in the 1940s and '50s. We would cup our
hands to our ears when the Old Woman feigned deaf-
ness and throw our hands in the air on the last line.
You can expand this by adding other household tasks
for the gentleman to enquire about: "Are you fond of
cooking?," etc.

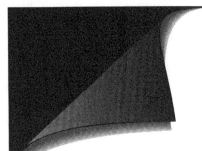

Story Finger Plays
for the Very Young

*From U.S. and Canadian Librarians
and Teachers*

When working with preschool children, finger-play stories are useful short fillers. They provide a little stretch between tales. I have even seen skillful tellers like Sherry Norfolk simply flip into a finger play like "Tommy Thumbs Up" right in the middle of another story as a way to get squirming kids back on focus. She didn't miss a beat, just picked the story back up and kept on going. The kids who had been distracted by folks strolling past our tent were all face-front and listening again. Jane Cobb's *I'm a Little Teapot* (cited below) is an excellent source for many, many story finger plays.

Tommy Thumbs Up

■ 20 seconds

Tommy Thumbs up and   Thumbs up.
Tommy Thumbs down.   Thumbs down.
Tommy Thumbs dancing   Dance thumbs to right.
all around the town.   Dance thumbs to left.

Dance 'em on your shoulders.
Dance 'em on your head.

Dance 'em on your knees and
tuck them into bed.   Fold arms and tuck thumbs into armpits.

> ▌ This can be repeated using "Toby Tall" (middle finger), "Ring Man"
> ▌ (ring finger), "Baby Fingers" (pinkie), and "Finger Family" (all fingers).

This finger play is popular among preschool caregivers. It is included in *I'm a Little Teapot! Presenting Preschool Storytime* by Jane Cobb (Vancouver: Black Sheep Press, 1996), p. 83.

Way Up High in the Apple Tree

■ 16 seconds

Way up high in the apple tree   Stretch arms to sky.
two little apples looked at me.   Make circles with fingers to show apples.
I shook that tree as hard as I could, Shake tree.
and down fell the apples.   Fingers show apples falling.
Mmmm, were they good!   Take a bite and rub tummy.

This finger play is popular with teachers in the fall. This text is from *Booksharing: 101 Programs to Use with Preschoolers* by Margaret Read MacDonald (Hamden, Connecticut: Library Professional Publications, 1988), p. 65.

Five Little Jack-o-lanterns

■ 35 seconds

Five little jack-o-lanterns, sitting on a gate.   Five fingers upright.
The first one said, "It's getting late."   First finger wiggles.
Second one said, "There're witches in the air."   Second finger wiggles.
Third one said, "I don't care."   Third finger wiggles.
Fourth one said, "Let's have some fun."   Fourth finger wiggles.
Fifth one said, "Let's run and run and run."   Fingers run back and
                                                   forth in air.

Oooooh went the wind.
OUT went the light.   Clap on "out."
And five little jack-o-lanterns rolled out of sight!   Hand runs behind back.

From *Booksharing: 101 Programs to Use with Preschoolers* by Margaret Read MacDonald (Hamden, Connecticut: Library Professional Publications, 1988), p. 99.

Miss Polly Had a Dolly

■ 30 seconds

Miss Polly had a dolly who was sick, sick, sick.   Rock in arms.
Called for the doctor, "Come quick, quick, quick."   Phone to ear.
Doctor came with his bag and his hat.   Hold bag, tip hat.
Knocked on the door with a rat-a-tat-a-tat.   Knock.
Looked at the dolly, and he shook his head.   Shake head.
He said, "Miss Polly, put her straight to bed."   Shake finger.
He wrote on a paper for a pill, pill, pill.   Mime writing.
"I'll be back in the morning with my bill, bill, bill."

Found in *I'm a Little Teapot! Presenting Preschool Storytime* by Jane
Cobb (Vancouver: Black Sheep Press, 1996), p. 187. For six other
sources, see *Creative Fingerplays and Action Rhymes: An Index and
Guide to Their Use* by Jeff Defty (Phoenix: Oryx, 1992).

Short Folktales for Any Age

The tales in this section have wisdom that appeals to adults and fantasy to delight children, too.

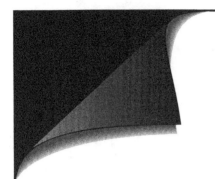

The Young Reader
A Folk Legend from India
As told by Manorama Jafa

1 minute, 45 seconds

Kapil Dev loved to read.
Everywhere he went he had a book in his hands.

"Kapil, go fetch your father for dinner."

"Yes, Mother."

Kapil started down the path to the fields to fetch his father.
His bare feet found their way along the path by themselves
because Kapil was deeply engrossed in his book.

Suddenly—"*Ouch!*" Kapil stubbed his toe on a rock in the path.
Kapil stopped and rubbed his toe.
Then he picked up his book and went on down the path . . . still reading.

"*Ouch!*" It happened again.
The hazards of reading!

Now, Saraswati, the Goddess of Learning, was watching all of this.
She made herself appear on the path in front of him.
But Kapil, still reading, walked right by without even noticing.

"Kapil?" she whispered in his ear. "I am here."

Still he didn't notice.

"*Kapil!* It is *I*, the Goddess of Learning."

Kapil looked up, stunned.
He bowed respectfully to the goddess. The book was still between his hands.

"I am pleased with you, Kapil," smiled the goddess.
"You are a true son of learning.
Even though you hurt your feet . . . .you keep right on reading.
I would like to grant you a favor.
Is there anything you would like to ask for?"

"Oh, yes!" Kapil knew exactly what he wanted.
"Could I have an eye, please, in each of my feet?
Then I could walk and read at the same time with no problem!"

The goddess laughed.
"Yes, Kapil.
A scholar-to-be such as you could certainly use another pair of eyes.
It is *done.*"

Kapil looked down.
"Perfect!" He now had an eye on each foot.
"Thank you, thank you, dear goddess."

Off Kapil went, down the path and through the fields.
Reading . . . reading . . .
but never stubbing his toe again!

Kapil Dev became one of the most learned sages in all of India.
And because of the eyes on his feet, he was given another name,
Chakshupad.
In the Sanskrit language this means "man with eyes on his feet."

Retold from *Golden Tales from India* by Manorama Jafa
(New Delhi: Khaas Kitaab Foundation, 2002), pp. 1-3.
I heard Manorama tell this delightful little tale at the
Asian Storytelling Congress in Singapore in 2002.
Thanks to Manorama Jafa for permission to retell
it here.

The Maiden in Green
A Chinese Folktale

| 1 minute

At a temple high in the mountains,
a young student was studying late into the night.
Practicing his calligraphy,
he became drowsy and fell asleep.

In his sleep he dreamed a dream.
A beautiful maiden in a green silk dress appeared before him.
She was trembling, in great distress.
"Save me! Save me!" she pleaded.
And then she vanished.

He awoke with a start.
The dream had seemed so real.

Then he became aware of a buzzing noise behind him.
He turned . . . and there in the open window he saw a large spider-web.
Entangled in the web was a little green bee.
Approaching the bee, closer and closer, was a large, hungry spider!

The student jumped up to break the web and chase off the spider.
He gently removed the little bee from the sticky web
and laid it on his ink-stone.
He marveled at the beauty of the little green creature.

Slowly the bee began to recover.
Then it walked down the ink-stone and waded into the ink.
With a little hop, it jumped down onto his blank writing paper.
The bee began to waddle about on the paper, as if it were doing a little dance.
Then the bee spread its wings and flew out the open window.

70

The student stared at the paper.
With its inky little feet,
the bee had written the character for "Thank you!"

Retold from "The Maiden in Green" by Berta
Metzger in *Picture Tales from the Chinese* (Philadelphia:
J.B. Lippincott, 1934), pp. 56-57.

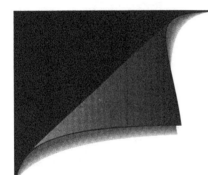

The Yu Player
from the South
A Chinese Folktale

1 minute, 35 seconds

There was once a king in China who loved the sound of the yu.
This unusual instrument had thirty-six reed pipes.
The harmony of a chorus of yu playing was indeed wonderful.

This king sent for 300 yu players to assemble in his palace.
The yu players came from all over the kingdom.
Some from the west,
some from the east,
some from the north,
some from the south.

And when those 300 yu players began to play . . .
the music was so amazing that listeners wept at its beauty.

But among those 300 yu players
there was one man from the south
who could not play a single note!

He had heard of the call for yu players,
so he had come with the players from the south to the king's palace.
He was quite happy living in the palace.
He could eat the king's fine food and laze around all day.
When it was time to play
he would lift his yu to his lips and pretend to play and play.
In the huge crowd of yu players . . .
no one noticed that no sound came from his yu.

But he was caught out, as always happens.

The king died. And a new king took the throne.
The yu players feared that they might be dismissed.
But it was not so.
"I love yu music just as well as the former king," said the new king.
"But I love the solo yu.
I would like each of you to play a concert for me in turn.
There are 300 of you. So I shall have a new concert each day for 300 days."

And so he did . . .
for 299 days, that is.
On the 300th day no yu player appeared.

The yu player from the south had gone south.

To this day, it is said of someone who pretends to do a thing of which he is
not capable . . . "Oh, him? He's just a man from the south."

Retold from "The Man from the South" in *Picture
Tales from the Chinese* by Berta Metzger (Philadelphia:
J.B. Lippincott, 1934), pp. 81–82; and "The Man Who
Pretended He Could Play Reed Pipes" in *Yue Yin
Suen (Selected Fables)* (Beijing: New World Publishing),
2002, p. 143. I found another interesting variant of
this story at www.hanyu.com. It places the story during the Warring States Period (475–221 BC). The king
of the state of Qi had a band of 300 yu players. A man
named Nanguo joined the band, even though he
could not play well. From this story comes the phrase,
"Be there just to make up the number." This is used
to mock someone passing for a specialist but is also
used by people self-referentially to show their mod-
esty. The yu is an ancient instrument similar to the
shêng, which is still used in Chinese music, but
smaller in size. It consists of a group of bamboo
pipes bound into a circular instrument and blown
through a wind spout that sticks out of the base
of the instrument. A photo can be found at
http://trfn.clpgh.org/free-reed/history/sheng/html.

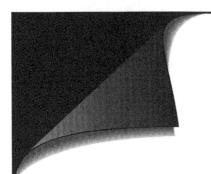

How Two Water Snakes Moved House

A Chinese Fable

▪ 30 seconds

Two snakes needed to move from a marsh which was drying up.

"I'll lead the way, and you follow," said the larger snake.

"That is not a good idea," said the smaller snake. People will see you, with me following behind. They will know we are moving and someone will kill you.
Let me ride on your back.
Then they will think I am a God.
Each should hold the other's tail in his mouth.
People will be afraid to harm us."

And so the snakes joined together and began to cross the highway.

It was just as the smaller snake had said.
People stared in amazement.
"Look! It is magic!
Make way for the magical snakes!"

And so they crossed the road.

Retold from "How Two Water Snakes Moved House" in *Yue Yin Suen (Selected Fables)* (Beijing: New World Publishing, 2002), pp. 149-151. Motif B765 *Fanciful qualities of snakes.*

The Story Not Told, the Song Not Sung

A Folktale from India

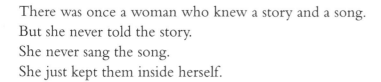

1 minute, 45 seconds

There was once a woman who knew a story and a song.
But she never told the story.
She never sang the song.
She just kept them inside herself.

The song and story felt neglected inside that woman for so long.
One afternoon when she was napping,
The story jumped out of her open mouth and escaped.
The story took the form of a pair of men's shoes and sat down outside the door.
The song had also escaped.
It took the form of a man's coat and hung itself on a peg.

When the woman's husband came home, he was surprised.
"Who is visiting?"

"No one," said his wife.

"Then to whom do this coat and these shoes belong?"

The wife was at a loss to explain.

The husband went off in a rage to sleep at the Monkey God's temple that night.

The woman sat there for a long while trying to puzzle this out.
"Where could those shoes and the coat have come from?
At last she lay down and put out the lamp.

Now all of the lamp flames of the town, once they are put out at night,
go to the Monkey God's temple to gossip.

On this night one of the flames was late arriving.

"Why were you so late tonight?"

"Oh, my couple quarreled tonight.
The husband came home to find a man's coat on the peg.
And there was a pair of man's shoes by the door."

"No wonder he was angry!" said the other flames.

"But it wasn't what he thought.
His wife knew a song that she never sung.
She knew a story that she did not tell.
The story escaped and turned itself into a pair of shoes.
The song escaped and turned itself into a coat.
They took their revenge on that woman.
Of course she knows nothing about this."

The husband was lying in the Monkey God's temple all this time.
He pretended to be asleep,
but he heard everything the flames said.

In the morning he went home and apologized to his wife.
Then he asked her to tell her story and sing her song.

"What story?" she said.
"What song?"

Both were gone.

Retold from "A Story and a Song" in *A Flowering Tree and Other Oral Tales from India* by A.K. Ramanujan (Berkeley: University of California Press, 1997), pp. 1-2. MacDonald classifies this tale under Motif M231.1 *Free keep in an inn exchanged for good story.* That tale sometimes occurs in conjunction with the motif of refusal to tell stories. Under M231.1B★ *Man with no tale sees story spirits* MacDonald cites tales from Russia, Korea, and Rumania. MacDonald and Sturm cite Korean and Cambodian variants. Also Motif N454.2 *King overhears conversation of lamps.*

Riddle Tales

Most riddle tales can be told in under three minutes. For an extremely useful selection of these
stories see George Shannon's five collections
—*Stories to Solve, More Stories to Solve, Still More
Stories to Solve, True Lies, and More True Lies* (full
citation data provided in the bibliography at the
end of the book). His riddle stories are written
so that the teller can set up the riddle, leaving the
audience to guess the answer. Eventually the
teller reveals the ending. If you are working under
a three-minute deadline, though, you may have
to truncate the audience's guessing time.

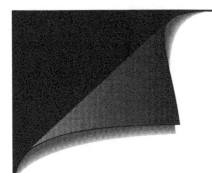

Thief and Master-Thief
A Folktale from India

 1 minute, 45 seconds, excluding
guessing time

A town once had two thieves.
One thief was called Master-Thief.
But he was a skinny fellow, not good in a fight.
The second thief was strong. But he was called merely Thief.
He was jealous of Master-Thief and wanted that title for himself.

One night both men went to a nearby town to rob houses.
Master-Thief broke into a rich man's house and stole ten thousand rupees.
Thief saw Master-Thief coming down the street with bulging pockets.
Here is where I prove my superiority, he thought.
I am going to rob Master-Thief!

"What a hard night's work," he called to Master-Thief.
"Why don't we share a room at the hostel tonight.
It's too late to go all the way back home."

Master-Thief agreed.
As soon as Master-Thief was asleep,
Thief got up silently and went through all of Master-Thief's pockets.
There was no money there.
He checked cautiously under the blankets.
No money.

Thief went to bed unhappily.
Where could Master-Thief have hidden those rupees?

Next morning the two thieves agreed to spend another day in this town.
They would meet in the evening and spend the night together once more.

Once more Master-Thief returned with bulging pockets.
Thief could hardly wait until Master-Thief fell asleep.
Then he began to go through Master-Thief's things once again.
No money.
He searched the cracks in the wall of the room.
He even went outside and poked around in the rafters.
He looked under the bushes near the hostel.
No money.

In the morning Thief was too frustrated.
He had to ask.
"Master-thief, where do you hide your money at night?"

"There is an art to thievery," said the Master-Thief.
"I knew you would try to rob me.
So I hid my money in a place you would never think to look."

▌ Let audience guess where he hid it.

Master-Thief smiled.

"I hid it under *your* bed."

Thief smiled too..
"You deserve the title of Master-Thief!"
And Thief bowed to the Master.

Retold from *A Flowering Tree and Other Oral Tales from India* by A.K. Ramanujan (Berkeley: University of California, 1997), p. 190. *Type 1525 The Master Thief.*

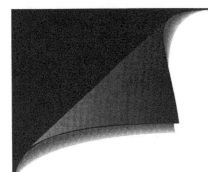

The Hare
and the Lion King

A Fable from Burma

■▐ 1 minute, 30 seconds, excluding
guessing time

The Lion King always wanted to hear praise from his advisors.
He surrounded himself with advisors who would give him nothing
but praise.

One day the Lion King noticed that everyone was backing away when
he spoke.
I wonder if I have bad breath, he thought.

So he called the jackal to his side.

"Dear Jackal," said the King.
"Do I by any chance have bad breath today?"

The jackal was nearly blown away by the bad breath of the king.
Forgetting himself, he spoke truthfully.

"Whew! Your majesty has *really* bad breath today!"

"Is that so?"

And with one blow of his huge paw . . .
The Lion King did away with the jackal.

"Fox, come here.
I need your advice.
Tell me, is my breath bad today?"

The fox had seen what happened to the jackal.
So he responded quickly . . .
"Oh no, your majesty.
Your breath is a sweet as a field of flowers."
It was obvious that the fox was just trying to flatter the king.

The King glared at the fox.
"I cannot stand a liar!" he cried.
And with another swipe of his huge paw
He put an end to the fox.

"Rabbit! Come here!
I need a trusted advisor.
Now tell me the truth.
Is my breath foul or fresh today?"

The little rabbit was trembling.
He had seen exactly what happened to the jackal and the fox.

After thinking for a moment,
The rabbit replied . . . .

> To set this story up as a riddle, stop here and ask,
> "What do you think the rabbit said?"

"Oh your majesty . . . .
I am sorry to say that I have a terrible cold today.
I cannot smell a thing.
So I am unable to judge in this matter."

MacDonald J811.2.1★ *Lion asks for judgment of his
breath. Sheep tells truth, wolf flatters—both killed. Fox
has a cold can't smell.* MacDonald cites sources from
Burma (Shan) and Aesop. Stith Thompson cites a
Spanish variant.

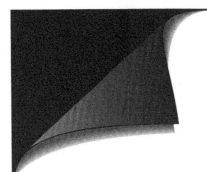

Pig and Bear
in Big Business

A Folktale from Czechoslovakia

1 minute, 15 seconds, excluding
guessing time

Pig and Bear decided to open food stalls.
Pig baked potatoes.
Bear fried a batch of doughnuts.

They took their food down to the marketplace and set up shop.

Pretty soon Bear got hungry.
"Say Pig, how much are you selling those potatoes for?"

"Five cents."

"Well I'll take one," said Bear.
He happended to have five cents in his pocket.
So he lumbered over with his coin.

Pig had made one sale already.
Now that he had some cash, he decided to treat himself.

"How much are your doughnuts, Bear?"

"Five cents."

"Great! I've already earned five cents!"
So Pig bought a doughnut from Bear.

Now Bear was feeling really good. He had made a sale already today.
He decided to have another baked potato.

He walked over to Pig's stall, gave him five cents,
and walked back munching the potato.

It wasn't long before Pig began to feel hungry again.
He had five cents and he'd already made two sales this day.
So he treated himself to another doughnut.

By then it was almost noon, and Bear was hungry.
So of course he had to have another potato.

And so it went.

At the end of the day the two friends counted their money.
They had each sold all of their stock.
And yet between them they still had only a nickel!

How could this be?

Inspired by "How the Pig and the Bear Went into
Business" in *Twelve Iron Sandals and Other Czechoslovak
Tales* by Vít Horejs (Englewood Cliffs, New Jersey:
Prentice-Hall, 1985) and by a performance by Seattle
teller Jennifer Irwin, who tells the story with Pig tossing the hot potatoes from hand to hand and mutter-
ing "Hotty hotty hotty!" while Bear throws his
doughnuts into the sizzling oil with a *slap . . . slap . . .
szzzz!* This is Motif B294 *Animals in business relations.*

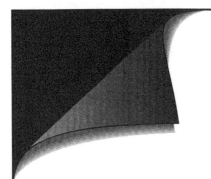

The Parrot
and the Parson
A European Folktale

There was once a parrot who was kept in a golden cage by a banker.
Everyday the banker would command that the parrot talk to him.
Though the parrot repeatedly asked the banker to let him fly free,
the banker always refused.

One day the parson came to visit.
When the parson came near the cage to admire the bird,
the parrot spoke to him.
"I want to fly free.
Can you help me escape from this cage?"

The parson felt sorry for the poor bird.
He could not release the banker's bird.
But he nodded at the parrot and winked.

Then the parson took two steps backward and fell over in a dead faint.

The banker raced to help the parson.

Next day the parrot escaped.

How did he do this?

Take guesses from the audience.

Answer: The parson showed him what to do by fainting. The next day the
parrot lay down on the floor of his cage, stuck his feet in the air, and did

not move. The banker assumed he was dead, so he threw the bird out onto the dust heap and the parrot flew free.

Retold from "The Parrot and the Parson" in *Just One More* by Jeanne B. Hardendorff (Philadelphia: J.B. Lippincott, 1969), pp. 49-51. Her source was *The Talking Thrush* by W.H.D. Rouse (New York: J.M. Dent, 1899). In *The Subtleties of the Inimitable Mulla Nasrudin* by Idries Shah (New York: E.P. Dutton, 1973) the parrot sends another bird to tell his family he has been trapped. One of his family members falls dead (feigning), and when the bird returns with this news the parrot knows how to escape. Motif K522.4 *Captive parrots in net play dead and are thrown out: escape.* Thompson cites one source from India. MacDonald K522.4.0.1★ *Parrot has parson ask lawyer how to escape from cage.* MacDonald cites a Tatar variant. Also in MacDonald are a Hungarian variant in which a cock eats gold and feigns death, a Finnish variant in which a fox trapped in a pit feigns death, a Ceylonese variant in which a peacock feigns death, and a Joel Chandler Harris tale in which a fox trapped in a hollow tree feigns death.

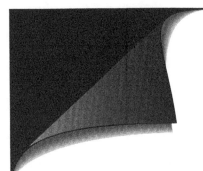

The Clever Old Woman of Carcassonne

A French Legend from Languedoc

1 minute, 40 seconds, excluding guessing time

Carcassonne had been under siege for a long, long time.
The food was almost all gone.
The people were sick and hungry.
It seemed that they must give up in defeat.

It was announced that Carcassonne would surrender the next day.

But one old woman could not accept this.
"No!" she shouted from the crowd.
"Try one more thing before we surrender.
I have an idea that may work."

"I need just two things," said the old woman.
"I need a cow.
I need a bushel of grain."

At first it seemed that there was no cow to be found in Carcassone.
But it turned out that one old miser had been hiding a cow all this time.

The cow was brought to the old woman.

"Now the bushel of grain.
To feed to the cow."

Everyone cried out in an uproar!
"Feed it to the cow?
That is the last of our grain, and we are so hungry!"

But when the woman told them her plan . . .
they agreed.

What do you think her plan was?

> Let the audience guess at this point. If they do not guess,
> or guess in part, tell the rest of the tale.

The old woman fed the entire bushel of grain to the cow.
During the night, she had the gate opened just a crack and pushed the
cow out.

In the morning the soldiers besieging the castle saw the cow
wandering about.
Believing the citizens of Carcassonne must have let the cow out to graze,
they captured it and brought it to their king.

"Kill the cow and we will have meat tonight!" the king ordered.

But when the cow was butchered, it was found that its stomach was full
of grain.

"The people of Carcassonne still have so much grain they can feed it to
their livestock!
We would have to wait here for months before they surrender.
We have not enough supplies for such a long siege."

So the king and his troops broke camp and moved off.
Thus Carcassonne was saved
because of one wise old woman.

Retold from "The Clever Old Woman of
Carcassonne" in *Picture Tales from the French* by
Simone Chamoud (Philadelphia: J.B. Lippincott,
1933), pp. 24-27. Motif K2365.1 *Enemy induced to
give up siege by pretending to have plenty of food.*
Thompson cites sources from Herodotus, Ovid,
Spain, Japan, Grimm, and other German sources.

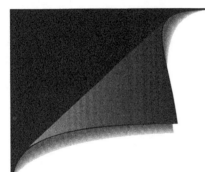

The Fool at the Country Store

A True Story from Southern Indiana

1 minute, excluding guessing time

There used to be a young feller who hung out at the country store
all the time.
It seemed he wasn't too bright.
So the men had a lot of fun out of him.
They'd tease him about this and that,
and they'd try to think up ways to play tricks on him.

They developed a really funny game that they liked to play with him.
A man would hold out his hands with a coin in the palm of each.
One would be a dime.
One would be a nickel.

"Now pick the one you want," the man would say.
"You can have whichever one you choose.
Do you want the big one or the little one?"

The boy would stare at the two hands for a long time.
Scratch his head.
It seemed like he never could make up his mind.
Then finally . . . he would take the nickel.
He always took the nickel.

The men sitting around in the store would laugh and laugh at the stupid kid.

My friend Spiv Helt told me about this.

He said, "When you think about it . . . he might not have been as stupid as
they all thought."

Why do you think Spiv came to that conclusion?

■ Let the audience guess.

Answer: If he had taken the dime, they would have stopped teasing him with the game.

My source is Gordon "Spiv" Helt, Scipio, Indiana. Gordon told this as a true story, and I believe it was, since he told several stories about this same young man. Interestingly, a similar story appears in *Stories of the Spirit, Stories of the Heart: Parables of the Spiritual Path from Around the World,* edited by Christina Feldman and Jack Kornfield (San Francisco: HarperSanFrancisco, 1991), p. 275. It is cited as a Sufi story and told with Mulla Nasrudin as the dolt.

Humorous Tales

There is always a place in the repertoire for short, humorous tales. Those given here are gentle-smile tales, not belly-laugh jokes. (For the latter, there are many collections of jokelore available.) It is interesting to note that many of the humorous anecdotes being told today were also being told hundreds of years ago.

Teaching the Horse to Speak
A Folktale from Turkey

▌ 45 seconds

The hodja once went to the king and offered to teach the king's horse to talk.
"Are you sure you can do this?" asked the king.

"I am certain of it," assured the hodja.
"But it will take time.
I believe I can train this horse in just six years.
But I will need one hundred gold pieces to feed and care for the horse while it is learning."

The king really wanted to see this wonder of a talking horse.
So he handed over to the hodja his best horse *and* one hundred pieces of gold.

The hodja went home happily.
"But aren't you worried?" asked his friend.
"If this horse can't talk in six years' time, the king will behead you."

"Oh, I am not worried," replied the hodja.
"In six years time a lot can happen.
I might die.
The king might die.
Or the horse might die."

For sources see p. 94

Talking Turkeys
A Folktale from Syria

1 minute, 30 seconds

One Syrian woman was even cleverer than the hodja.
Seeing that the queen had a large flock of turkeys, the woman
approached her.
"Your Majesty, I don't know if you are aware of this.
Your turkeys are of a rare breed. They are capable of human speech.
I myself know how to train these turkeys.
If you will let me take them to my home, I will teach them not one,
but *seven* wonderful languages.
And I can do all this in just sixty nights."

The queen did not believe this possible, but she agreed to let the woman try.
It would be a wondrous thing if it proved to be true.

"I will, of course, need provisions for these remarkable birds," said the woman.
"I will need one hundred bags of flour, ten baskets of nuts, ten baskets of
sugar, twenty baskets of dates . . . ." And the woman went on to name all of
the rich foodstuffs of which she could think.

The queen provided everything the woman asked, and the woman had it
all taken to her home along with the turkeys.

For sixty days she ate pastries and every good thing she could make from
those wonderful ingredients.
The turkeys she let peck for themselves in the yard.

At the end of the sixty days, the woman hurried to the queen.
"Your Majesty, a terrible thing is happening!
Those turkeys of yours have learned to talk all right.
But they are saying strange things.

They keep calling out. . . . 'The queen has a lover! The queen has a lover!'
What am I to do?"

The queen turned pale.
"Go at once and kill those turkeys!
Don't bring them anywhere near the palace!"

So the woman went home and did as the queen had ordered.
She killed a turkey every week until they were all gone . . .
and roasted and ate them too.

This is Motif K491 *Trickster paid to educate an ass. He
gets paid in advance. He gradually starves the ass.* Stith
Thompson cites versions from Germany, Turkey
(Hodscha Nasreddin), and India. Thompson gives
Italian and Indian variants for Motif K491.1 *Trickster
paid to teach monkey to talk.* He has one Indian variant
for K491.2 *Horse to be taught to speak.* Also see Motif
K551.11 *Ten year respite given while captive undertakes to
teach elephant (ass) to speak. Captive explains to friends
that in that time the captor, the elephant (ass), or himself is
likely to die.* Thompson cites an Italian novella with
this theme. This story is also told of Tyl Ulenspiegel,
who tricks the rector of Erfurt University, saying he
can teach an ass to read and write. MacDonald cites a
Flemish version and an Italian variant. Also Motifs
K1958 *Sham teacher,* and H1024.4 *Task: teaching an ass
to read.* Related to Tale Type 1675 *The Ox (Ass) as
Mayor.* A version of "The Talking Turkeys" may be
found in *Arab Folktales* by Inea Bushnaq (New York:
Pantheon, 1986), pp. 325-326. She cites this as a
Syrian tale but does not give a specific source.

The Dripping Nose
An Anecdote from Southern Indiana

■ 30 seconds

Down in Southern Indiana where I come from they tell this tale.

There was a young feller went courtin' his girlfriend.
Her folks brought him into the sitting room and they all sat around
making small talk.
They sat and sat.
Pretty soon his nose started to run.
He'd forgotten to bring along a handerchief and didn't know just what to do.
He snuffled a while.
Looked around the room.
Suddenly he had a bright idea.

"Say! I think *that* picture over there . . .
would look a lot better over *there*!"

> The teller mimes wiping his nose with his sleeves while pointing first to
> the left and then to the right. His index finger runs under his nose while
> pointing to the left, then his sleeve wipes the nose as it follows his finger.

A jest widely known throughout the U.S. From the
author's mother, Mildred Amick, of Jennings County,
Indiana.

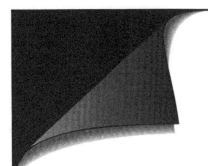

The Learned Scholar
A Jewish Folktale

1 minute, 15 seconds

A learned scholar from the University of Constantinople was crossing the
Black Sea in a small boat.
Feeling very full of himself, he struck up a conversation with the boatman.
"Tell me, my good man, what is your opinion of philosophy?"
The boatman was bewildered.
"I'm afraid I have no opinion, sir. I have never studied philosophy."

"Never studied *philosophy*? Terrible! Terrible!
Than a fourth of your life has been wasted!" exclaimed the scholar.

After a while the scholar brought up another topic.
"Well then, what is your opinion of history?"

The boatman shrugged.
"History also I have never studied."

"Never studied *history?* Terrible! Terrible!
Then I would have to say that two-fourths of your life has been wasted!"

The scholar was silent for a while, and then he began again.

"Well then, *science.* Surely you have studied *science.*"

"No sir. Science is another thing I have never studied."

"No science! Terrible! Terrible!
Then one must say that three-fourths of your life has been wasted!"

Before the scholar could pose another question, the winds began to rise.
Suddenly the waves broke harshly over the boat and the small vessel capsized.

"Swim for your life, professor!" called the boatman, as a huge wave swept him away.
"We are not far from shore."

"But . . . I never learned to swim!" called the terrified scholar.

"What? Terrible! Terrible!" shouted the boatman.
"Then one must say that *four-fourths* of your life is now wasted!"

Retold from the delightful version in Rose Dobbs' *More Once-Upon-a-Time Stories* (New York: Random House, 1961), pp. 39-42. Dobbs found this story in *Ivrit Hayyah (Modern Hebrew)* by Dr. Harry Blumberg and Mordecai H. Lewittes (New York: Hebrew Publishing Co, 1946). Motif J1217 *Worldly man puts religious man out of countenance.* MacDonald classifies this as J1229.4★ *Pedagogue asks ferryman if he has never studied grammar. "Then half your life has been wasted." Boat begins to sink. Ferryman asks pedagogue if he ever learned to swim. "Then all your life is lost."* An Iranian variant appears in Idries Shah, *The Exploits of the Incomparable Mulla Nasrudin* (London: Octagon, 1983). The tale also appears in Heather Forest, *Wisdom Tales from Around the World* (Little Rock: August House, 1996), p. 57.

Moving the Stone
A Turkish Folktale

■ 35 seconds

The hodja once saw several young boys arguing about which of them was the strongest.
There was a large stone in the middle of the village, and the boys always competed to see who would be strong enough to move it a little.

This day, none had succeeded.

"Let me have a try!" called the hodja.

"What? You are an old man!" the youths taunted.
"What strength could you have?"

"I may be old," retorted the hodja.
"But I am still just as strong as I was in my youth!
Stand aside!"

And the hodja put his shoulder to the stone and began to push.
He pushed . . . and pushed . . . and pushed . . .

Then the hodja laughed.

"It is just as I told you.
I am still as strong as I was in my youth.
I couldn't move it then *either.*"

Another version appears in *The Subtleties of the Inimitable Mulla Nasrudin* by Idries Shah (New York: Dutton, 1973). For a version set up as a riddle tale, see *More True Lies: Eighteen Tales for You to Judge* by George Shannon (New York: Greenwillow, 2001), pp. 19-21. Motif H1562.2 *Test of strength: lifting stone.*

The Man and The Lion Travel Together

A Fable of Aesop

■ 35 seconds

A man and a lion were traveling together.
The lion started to brag.
"What a puny little thing you are, man.
Don't you wish you were strong like a lion?"

But man was not intimidated.

"Strong? A man is much stronger than a lion!"

They went on, arguing about who was the strongest.

There beside the road was a carved stone statue.
It depicted a muscular young man strangling a lion.

"See!" said the man.
"There you have the proof!
Man is much stronger than a lion!"

The lion cocked his head and looked at the statue.

"If lions knew how to carve," he said,
"You would see a different victim."

Retold from "The Man and the Lion Traveling
Together" in *Aesop Without Morals* by Lloyd W. Daly
(New York: Thomas Yoseloff, 1961), p. 284, and from a
telling by Beatrice Garrard, New Year's Eve, 2003.

The Best Part of All
A Contemporary Anecdote

■ 30 seconds

A little boy came home from school very excited.
"I got the best part in the school play!" he announced.

"Are you the prince?" queried his mother.

"No! Better than that!"

"You must be playing the part of the king."

"Oh, no. Better than that too!"

The mother knew they were producing a play of The Frog Prince.

"Well, my goodness. You must be the frog!"

"Oh, no . . . way better than that!"

"Well what part are you playing?
I can't guess."

"I have the most wonderful part of all," exclaimed the little boy.
"I get to be the one who claps and cheers!"

This tiny tale was given to me by Seattle storyteller
Aarene Storm. I've been trying to shy away from run-
of-the-mill "heartwarming" stories here, as they are
available elsewhere. But this one does seem especially
pleasing to those of us in the performing arts.

The Tumblebug and the Eagle

A Folktale from Aesop

2 minutes, 15 seconds

Once a rabbit was being pursued by an eagle.
The rabbit took refuge with the tumblebug.
He begged the tumblebug to save him from the eagle.

The brave little tumblebug stood right up to the eagle.
"Do not touch this little rabbit!" he said.
"I am too small to stop you,
but in the name of Zeus I ask you not to harm this rabbit."

The eagle brushed the tumblebug aside with his wing
and gobbled up the rabbit.

The tumblebug was infuriated!
He flew after the eagle and saw where the eagle had his nest.
The next day, when the eagle was gone from the nest,
The tumblebug climbed up into the nest and
with great effort managed to roll the eggs out of the nest,
one at a time.
Each fell from the tree and was smashed on the rocks far below.

The eagle was beside himself with grief and fury when he returned.

Next season, the eagle built his nest high on a cliff.
But the tumblebug was not daunted.
He climbed until he reached the nest . . .
And pushed the eggs out!

The next year, the eagle did not dare lay his eggs anywhere on earth.
Instead he took the eggs to Olympus
and asked the great god Zeus to hold the eggs in his lap.
"Twice now my eggs have been destroyed on earth.
Someone wishes eagles to become extinct.
Please guard the eggs for me."
So Zeus agreed.

When the tumblebug saw this . . .
He went right to the dung pile and rolled up a ball of manure.
Flying to Olympus with the manure . . .
He dropped it right into the lap of Zeus.

"What?" Zeus jumped up to brush the dung off . . . .
and the eggs crashed to the ground.

Then Zeus ordered the tumblebug and eagle to come before him.

"I begged the eagle in your name, Zeus.
I asked that he not harm the rabbit who had sought my protection.
But the eagle ignored me and killed the rabbit."

"What you did was wrong," Zeus said to the eagle.
"The tumblebug is right to be angry."

"Now that the eagle has been punished," Zeus said to the tumblebug,
"you must leave him alone."

"Never!" exclaimed the tiny bug.
"I will not stop until the last eagle is extinct!"

When Zeus heard this he was concerned.
He did not want to lose the magnificent eagles from this world.
But neither did he want to extinguish the tiny tumblebug.

So Zeus changed the egg-laying season of the eagle.

Eagles now lay eggs only at a time of year when the tumblebugs are not around.

This way the two never meet.

Retold from *Aesop Without Morals* by Lloyd W. Daly (New York: Thomas Yoseloff, 1961), pp. 89-90, 94-95. The first variant is from a largely fictitious life of Aesop which is translated here by Daly. In this fiction, Aesop tells the story to the Delphians as they are about to throw him from a cliff, in a bid to sway them from killing him. Motif L315.7 *Dungbeetle keeps destroying eagle's eggs. Eagle at last goes to the sky and lays eggs in Zeus's lap. The dungbeetle causes Zeus to shake his apron and breaks the eggs.* See also A2457.1 *Why tumblebug rolls in dung.*

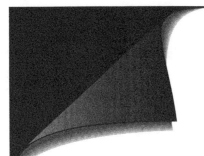

The Well-Read Frog
A Contemporary Anecdote

1 minute, 20 seconds

One day a chicken walked into a library.
The librarian was surprised to see a chicken coming in,
but she greeted it pleasantly.

The chicken walked right up to the counter and called,

"Book! Book! Book!"

"Why, that chicken can talk!" thought the librarian.
So she gave the chicken a book.
The chicken tucked the book under her wing
and marched out of the library.

The chicken wasn't gone long when she returned with the book.
She dropped it on the counter and began to call again,

"Book! Book! Book!"

"That chicken must be a fast reader!"

So the librarian found another book she thought the chicken might like
and helped her tuck it under her wing.
Off went the chicken.

But soon the chicken was back again.

"Book! Book! Book!"

This went on all day.

"That chicken can't be reading all those books," thought the librarian.
So she decided to follow the chicken and see what she was up to.

The next time the chicken took a book,
walked out of the library and down toward the pond ...
the librarian followed her.

When she got to the pond
the chicken held up the book and opened it.
A big frog jumped up on a lily pad.
That frog looked at the book for a moment.
Then the frog hollered,

"Read-it! Read-it! Read-it!"

This anecdote is often told by speakers at library con-
ferences. I have probably heard it told half a dozen
times in the last ten years. But, being a librarian, I still
love it! Caroline Feller Bauer includes a briefer version in her *New Handbook for Storytellers* (Chicago:
American Library Association, 1993), p. 173.

Scary Tales

Most scary tales require a bit longer than three minutes to build up suspense. But here is a selection of slightly scary tales that let ghosts, goblins, and other scary creatures do their work quite efficiently.

Look at My Teeth!
A Folktale from Cuba

▌▌ 2 minutes, 15 seconds

There was a man who always told tall tales.
No one believed a thing he said.
"You should have seen the fish I caught!
It was THIS long!
It had GREEN fins!
With GOLDEN gills!"

"Sure. Sure." People just ignored whatever he said.

One night this fellow was riding home alone late in the evening.
It happened to be a stormy night.
Lightning was crashing in the trees.
Thunder was rolling across the skies.

Suddenly his horse reared!

"What?"

There on the ground by the side of the road
was a grey bundle.

The man got down from his horse and examined it.
It was a very tiny baby!

"Someone has abandoned a child so far from home?
Well, I will have to take it back to the village."

He climbed back onto his horse and used his belt to strap the baby to
his back.
Off he rode.

After a while he felt something tapping him on the shoulder.

"*Tata! Tata!* Look at my teeth!
Tata! Tata! Look at my teeth!"

He turned around.

"Aaaahhh!" The baby opened its mouth wide.
He had a whole mouthful of teeth.

"This baby must be much older than I realized.
It must be a small child I have picked up."

The man kept on riding through the storm.
After a while he felt something poking him in the shoulder again.

"*Tata! Tata!* Look at my teeth!
Tata! Tata! Look at my teeth!"

The man turned.

"Aaahhh!" The baby opened its huge mouth!
Now it had teeth as large as those of a fully grown adult!

"What?"
The man spurred his horse faster.
"Something is not right with this child."

And once more . . . .

"*Tata! Tata!* Look at my teeth!
Tata! Tata! Look at my teeth!"

Dreading what he might see, the horseman turned.
The baby had teeth as big as a horse!

"Aaahhh!" The man *threw* the baby to the ground.
He galloped as fast as he could for the town.
At the inn no one believed his story at all.

"Sure. Sure. We know all about your tall tales."

But in the morning, when he was still trembling,
they agreed to go back with him
to the place where he had left the baby.

They didn't find any baby thrown on the ground there, that is for sure.
But after looking around for a while,
the man did notice a little black pig resting under a bush.

"Look at this little pig." He bent down to pet its sides.
The little pig looked up at him . . . .and opened its mouth!

"*Tata! Tata!* Look at my TEETH!"

Everyone saw this happen.

They say that in that village the man was never again accused of telling
tall tales.

Retold from "Los Dientes del Bebé" in *Maisí y Sus
Tradiciones Orales* by Luis Matos (Habana: Editorial
Letras Cubanas, 2002), pp. 7-9. Motifs G303.3.1.16
Devil appears as a child; D303.4.1.5 *Devil's teeth.* Matos
states in his preface that he began collecting these
stories in 1999. They are from the Maisí area. *Tata*
means "Daddy" here.

Squeak My Leg
A Folktale from Russia

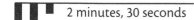 2 minutes, 30 seconds

An old man was going into the forest to chop wood one day
when his way was blocked by a huge bear.

"It's either you or me!" growled the bear.
"Leave the forest or we fight!"

The man had no intention of leaving the forest.
He threw his heavy axe and chopped the bear's hind leg right off!

The bear hobbled off into the woods snarling.

Then the man took that bear leg home and gave it to his wife.
"We can have bear stew for supper," he told her.

"And I will spin wool from the fur," said the woman.

They were delighted with their bear leg.

The old woman skinned the leg and put the meat on to boil.
Then she sat down on the hide and began to pluck off the fur and spin it
into wool.

But the bear had not given up.
He made himself a wooden leg.
And that night out of the forest he came.

The old couple could hear him chanting in the dark:

Squeak, my leg,
wooden leg.

Squeak my leg,
wooden leg.

Water sleeps.
Earth sleeps.
Village sleeps.
Farms sleep.
One old woman does not sleep.
On my hide she is sitting.
And my wool she is spinning.

Squeak, my leg,
wooden leg.
Squeak my leg,
wooden leg.

Water sleeps.
Earth sleeps.
Village sleeps.
Farms sleep.
One old man does not sleep.
On my meat, he is chawing.
On my bones, he is gnawing.

Squeak my leg,
wooden leg.

The old man and old woman heard that bear coming closer and closer.

Squeak, my leg,
wooden leg.

Then he BROKE DOWN THE DOOR AND GOBBLED THEM UP!
BOTH OF THEM!

And off into the forest he hobbled.

Squeak, my leg,
wooden leg.
Squeak, my leg,
wooden leg.

Water sleeps.
Earth sleeps.
Village sleeps.
Forest sleeps.
One old bear
now can sleep.

Retold from "The Bear" in *Russian Folklore: An Anthology in English Translation* by Alex E. Alexander (Belmont, Massachusetts: Nordland, 1975), pp. 206–207. This is related to Motif Z13.1 *Tale-teller frightens listener: yells "boo" at exciting point*, and to E235.4.1 *Return from dead to punish theft of golden arm from grave.* Tale Type 366 *Husband usually has taken it.* MacDonald's *Storyteller's Sourcebook* contains two U.S. variants of this tale: MacDonald E235.4.3.2★ *Man cuts off tail of critter and eats it. Creature returns for tail repeatedly. "You know, and I know, that I'm here to get my tailypo."* Also MacDonald Z13.1.2★ *The Old Woman and the Bear. Old woman on porch sings "Who'll spend the night with me?" Bear: "Me, by the corral." Etc. "My by the brush pile." "Me by the chimney corner." Jumps out and eats her up.*

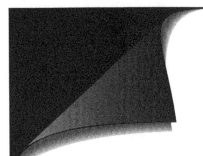

The Ghostly Sneeze
A Folktale from Picardy in France

1 minute, 35 seconds

It was once believed that the road to Englebelmer was haunted.
Travelers along the road would suddenly be startled by a violent
sneezing sound.

Achoo! Achoo! Achoo!

The traveler would stop . . . stare around . . . call out . . . "Who's there?"

But no one ever answered.
The traveler would start on down the road again.
But soon . . .

"Achoo! Achoo! Achoo!"

Word got around that a sneezing ghost haunted the road.
The ghost seemed to be teasing people,
following them along their way,
sneezing at them every time they began to feel they were safe again.

The people of the region eventually got used to the sneezing ghost.
Whenever he would start up with his *Achoo!* business,
they would just cross themselves and go on.

But one night a farmer was returning late from market
When the ghost started following him.

Achoo! Achoo! Achoo!

This went on for half an hour without letting up.
Finally the farmer could stand no more of it.

"Enough with your sneezing!" he shouted.
"May God bless you and your cold!"

Instantly the sneezing stopped
And a ghostly form appeared before him.

"Thank you, my friend," spoke the ghost.
"You have delivered me from this unending sneezing.
I was condemned to wander this road, sneezing, until some kind soul
should say to me, 'God bless you.'"

With that the ghost disappeared.
And if a sneeze was ever heard on that road again,
it was the sneeze of a human . . . not a ghost.

Next morning the farmer hurried to tell everyone in the village about this
good news.
And from then on, whenever anyone sneezed . . . everyone would shout,
"God bless you!"
And today . . . we still do!

Aaaaachooo!

"God bless you!"

Retold from "The Sneezer of Englebelmer" in
Picture Tales from the French by Simone Chamoud
(Philadelphia: J.B. Lippincott, 1933), pp. 40-44. Motif
A1537.1 *Origin of wishing long life to person who sneezes.*
Thompson cites a Buddhist source for this motif.
Another sneezing ghost is cited as Motif E552 *Ghost
in form of bear sneezes.*

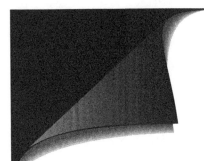

Painting Ghosts
A Chinese Tale

▪ 30 seconds

The prince of Qi had an artist in his employment.

"Tell me," asked the prince one day.
"What is the hardest thing to draw?"

"Dogs, horses—animals of any sort. They are very difficult to draw."

"What are the easiest things to draw?"

"Oh, ghosts and ogres!
Everyone sees dogs and horses every day and knows exactly what they
look like.
It is hard to draw them exactly as they are.
But ghosts and ogres? No one has ever seen them.
So they are easy to paint!"

Retold from "Painting Ghosts" in *Yue Yin Shen*
(Selected Fables) (Beijing: New World Publishing,
2002), p. 126. Motif F674 *Skillful painter. Can paint
from description of a dream* seems not quite to catch this
tale's intent.

Potato in My Hand

U.S. Folk Chant

 1 minute, 35 seconds

Little Boy was just getting into bed one night right near Halloween time. He had just pulled up the covers when he heard someone calling out from downstairs.

"I'm on the first step.
Here I stand.
I'm coming up the stairs
with a potato in my hand."

Little Boy pulled the covers up over his head.

"I'm on the second step.
Here I stand.
I'm coming up the stairs
with a potato in my hand."

Little Boy started shaking.

"I'm on the third step.
Here I stand.
I'm coming up the stairs
with a potato in my hand.

"I'm on the fourth step.
Here I stand.
I'm coming up the stairs
with a potato in my hand."

"I'm on the fifth step.
Here I stand.

I'm coming up the stairs
with a potato in my hand."

All the way up the stairs came the voice.

Then . . . .
"I'm in the hall.
Here I stand.
I'm coming down the hall
with a potato in my hand.

"I'm coming in the door.
Here I stand.
I'm coming in the door
with a potato in my hand."

Little Boy was just quaking under those covers.

"I'm standing by the bed.
Here I stand.
I'm standing by the bed
with a potato in my hand.

"TAKE IT!"

When Little Boy got the courage to pull down the covers and look around,
there was nothing there . . .
Just a big old potato lying at the foot of his bed!

I learned this from an educational music program for young children that was shown on public television in Seattle in the late 1970s. Let the audience join you on the chant. This one is more silly than creepy. In its story structure this is related to Motifs E235.4.1 *Return from dead to punish theft of golden arm from grave* and Z13.1 *Tale-teller frightens listener: yells "Boo" at exciting point.* Also Tale Type 366, but in this story the ghost leaves something rather than taking the terrified victim.

Stories to
Think About

These short stories are often called "wisdom tales." There is a list of sources for more such tales in the bibliography on page 159. These can be plugged into speeches, interspersed with longer tales in story programs, or told or read aloud in the classroom.

Tossing Starfish
A Speaker's Anecdote

50 seconds

A man was attending a conference at a seaside resort.
The first morning there he woke up early.
He took his coffee out onto his balcony to watch the sunrise.
The beach seemed to be glittering in the early morning light.
He decided to take a walk down to the beach.
When he reached the beach, he saw what had caused the glittering effect.
Hundreds of starfish had washed up during the night.
This was what he had seen from his window.

Suddenly he noticed a man moving along down by the water's edge.
The man was bending, picking up a starfish . . .
and tossing it far out into the water.

Walking down toward this starfish-tossing gentleman,
he called, "Don't you think this is an exercise in futility?
You can never save all of these starfish before the sun gets high."

The gentleman did not even pause in his task.
He bent, picked up another starfish, tossed it far,
and called back,
"Saved that one."

I first heard this anecdote at a Literary Lions Dinner
of the King County Library System in March 2000.
It was told by SeaFirst Bank executive Rosemary
Namit. Since then I have heard many versions.
Thanks to Rosemary for permission to use hers here.

A Storytelling Parable
A Modern Fable

█ 1 minute

There once was a man with wonderful stories.
Whenever his friends gathered, they would ask for his stories:
"Tell us the one about . . ."
They loved the way he told them.
They all knew how the stories went,
but no one else ever told them,
because they loved the way *he* told them.

Then the man began to travel.
He told his stories wherever he went.
Everyone loved them.

But after some years he returned to his home.
When he told his first story, they said, "Oh, that is the story Joseph tells."
When he told his second story, they said, "Oh, that is Esther's story."
All of his stories were being told by other people.

The man was very upset.
He went to the Wise Man of the village and complained.
"These have always been my stories.
Now everyone is telling them.
Don't they know the stories belong to me?
What can I do about this?"

"This is simple," said the Wise Man.
"Bring me your pillow."

When the man had brought his feather pillow,
The Wise Man held it high . . .
Then slit it open.

Feathers flew in every direction.
The wind carried some here, some there.
All down the street feathers were blowing away.

"What have you done?" cried the man.

"Your stories are like these feathers," replied the Wise Man.
"Once the story leaves your mouth,
it is carried away in the hearts of your listeners.
It no longer belongs to you."

"Is there nothing I can do?" worried the man.

"Oh yes," replied the Wise Man, watching the feathers drift down the road.
"You can let them go."

An original story by the author, based on the format of
the Jewish folktale in which a rabbi slits a pillow and
says that it is as easy to return the feathers blown away
on the wind as it is to recall gossiping words. For versions of that story see "Feathers" in *Doorways to the Soul*
by Elisa Davy Pearmain (Cleveland: Pilgrim Press,
1998), pp. 109-110; "The Gossip" by Marcia Lane in
Spinning Tales, Weaving Hope edited by Ed Brody et al.
(Philadelphia: New Society Publishers, 1992), p. 143;
and in *Wisdom Tales from Around the World* by Heather
Forest (Little Rock: August House, 1996), pp. 67-69. I
created this retelling of the old tale in order to make a
point I feel rather passionately about.

Rock vs. Plant

An Original Fable

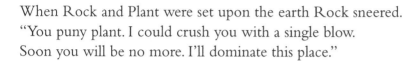

1 minute, 15 seconds

When Rock and Plant were set upon the earth Rock sneered.
"You puny plant. I could crush you with a single blow.
Soon you will be no more. I'll dominate this place."

But Plant smiled sweetly and said,
"We'll see. You, Rock, can never re-create.
I have the gift of growth. While you sit and wait . . . I'll creep and cover you."

"Just wait until I smash those tender tentacles!" Rock laughed.

But Plant stretched out in confidence. "You forget one thing, Rock.
You are inanimate. Rock cannot *move*."

Rock sat and sulked and sulked.
Until Man came along.
Man picked up Rock. He held Rock in his hand.
He raised Rock high and whacked a branch from Plant!

Rock laughed and called to Plant,
"Your end . . . inevitable!
Man sees in *me* a means to change the world and shape it to his will.
He'll never stop until the last green thing is dead.
He sees in *me* a tool to master all!"

To this day, Rock watches while man digs him out.
He uses Rock to make pavement, cement, asphalt . . . and force out Plant.

Of course as soon as Man has gone away . . .
Plant extends a tendril...then another . . .
and soon begins to cover Rock again.

But who will win? Which is inevitable?

An original fable by the author.

Quarreling Leads to Losses
A Fable from China

■ 45 seconds

An oyster was lying on the seashore one day with its shell open.
A greedy heron saw this and stuck his beak into the shell to eat the oyster.

But the oyster snapped his shell tight.
The heron's beak was caught.

"Let me go," hissed the heron through his trapped beak.
"No, I won't," muttered the oyster through his closed shell.

The heron was furious.

"If you don't open your shell today . . .
If you don't open your shell tomorrow . . .
There will be a dead oyster!"

But the oyster growled right back.
"If you can't take your beak out today . . .
If you can't take your beak out tomorrow . . .
There will be a dead heron!"

Just then a fisherman came down to the beach.
And since the two were so busy quarreling,
they were easily caught and popped into his bag.

"I see it is true," said the fisherman.
"Quarreling often leads to losses."

Retold from "The Oyster and the Heron" in *Picture Tales from the Chinese* by Berta
Metzger (Philadelphia: J.B.Lippincott, 1934), pp. 33-34. Another version, featuring mussel
and snipe, appears in *Peace Tales: World Folktales to Talk About* (New Haven, Connecticut:
Linnet Books, 1992), p. 33. This is Motif J219.1 *Enemies lose lives to a third party rather than
make peace*. MacDonald's *Storyteller's Sourcebook* cites two other Chinese variants (clam and
crane; oyster and heron). MacDonald/Sturm also cite a Chinese version (clam/crane).

The Argument Sticks

An Iroquois Tale

▌ 50 seconds

Two Iroquois brothers were arguing.
Neither would admit he was wrong.
They were about to come to blows over this.

Their mother gave them three sticks.

"These are special Argument Sticks.
They will solve this argument for you.
Set your sticks up in the woods,
leaning one against the other so they all stand up.
Leave them there for one month.
If they fall toward the north,
the one who set up the northern stick is right in this matter.
If they fall over toward the south,
the one who set up the southern stick is right in this matter."

The boys took their sticks into the woods and set them up.
They were satisfied that this would solve their argument.
A month later the boys remembered their Argument Sticks.
They went into the woods to find out who had won the argument.

The sticks had fallen in a heap and begun to rot.
There was no winner.

And the boys could not remember what the argument had been about in
the first place.

From "The Argument Sticks" in *Peace Tales: World Folktales to Talk About* by Margaret Read MacDonald (North Haven, Connecticut: Linnet Books, 1992), p. 87. Retold there from *Stories the Iroquois Tell Their Children* by Mabel Powers (New York: American Book Company, 1917), pp. 125-129.

In a Time Made Out of Twilight

A Poem-Tale
By Lenore Jackson

▌ 1 minute, 15 seconds

In a time made out of twilight
There was a land where the mountains pierced the sky.
And beyond the mountains a river flowed through silver willows
Passing meadows with scarlet poppies, fields of gold, and copper forests
Until at last it fell into the sea.

And in that sea there was an island
Where the pine trees touched the clouds
And ravens called from tree to tree
And looked down on a dragonfly gliding over bracken.

And under the bracken there was an acorn
And deep inside in that acorn, there stood a gnarled oak tree.
And in the shadow of that oak tree, a young man kissed a maiden.
And deep inside that young man's eyes was a little baby girl.

And in that baby's laughter was a wrinkled, white-haired woman
Who lived in a copper forest beyond the silver willows
And gathered scarlet poppies and put them in a basket
Where she kept a golden ring and a pearl beyond compare.

And that gnarled, white-haired woman threw that pearl into the sky
And it hung there like a moon, in a time made out of twilight.

This poem-tale is published here with permission of
the author, Seattle storyteller Lenore Jackson.

Plan of Attack

A Chinese Tale

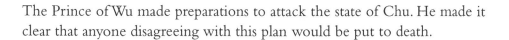

1 minute, 15 seconds

The Prince of Wu made preparations to attack the state of Chu. He made it clear that anyone disagreeing with this plan would be put to death.

One of his advisors felt strongly that commencing this war was not a good idea.
But he could not speak out.

Early one morning, the advisor took his slingshot and went strolling through the gardens.
He returned with his clothes wet with dew.
Each morning for three mornings he did this.

On the third morning, the prince asked him what he had been doing.
"Why are your clothes wet with dew every morning?
Where are you going so early?"

"I stroll through the garden with my slingshot," said the advisor.
"There is a tree in your garden on which a cicada lives.
The cicada clings to the tree, chirping away and drinking the dew.
It does not know that right behind it is a praying mantis.

"The praying mantis leans forward, its arms raised . . .
Ready to catch the cicada.
It does not know that right behind it perches a sparrow.

"The sparrow cranes its neck and prepares to snatch up the preying mantis.
It does not know that right behind it is a man with a slingshot.

"Those three small creatures are so intent on what is in front of them
That they fail to realize the danger that lies behind."

"Well spoken," said the prince.
And he gave up his plan of invasion.

Retold from "The Cicada, The Praying Mantis, and
the Sparrow" in *Yue Yin Suen (Selected Fables)* (Beijing:
New World Publishing, 2002), pp. 60-61.

The Old Man Who Moved Mountains

A Chinese Folktale

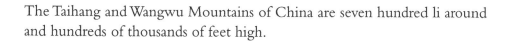

1 minute, 30 seconds

The Taihang and Wangwu Mountains of China are seven hundred li around and hundreds of thousands of feet high.

An old man who lived just north of the mountains found them quite in his way.
For all of his ninety years he had had to go far out of his way to get around those mountains whenever he wanted to travel.

He called his family together and set out a plan.

"Wouldn't it be fine if we could level down these mountains?" he suggested.
"We could open the road all the way through Yunan to Hanying.
We could all work together on this project."

His family all agreed.

But his wife thought it a poor idea.
"You haven't the strength to take down a small hill like Kuifu.
How could you ever move the Taihang and Wangwu Mountains?
And where would you dump all the earth and rocks?"

"We will dump them in the sea," the family answered.

So the old man set off with his son and grandson.
The dug up stones and earth,
loaded them into the baskets on their carrying poles,
and carried them clear to the tip of Bohai.

It took them from winter to summer to make the trip.

A wise man living at the river bend tried to stop them.
"This is nonsense!
An old man like yourself cannot even hope to carry away a huge mountain."

But the old man from the mountain just sighed and explained.

"I shall leave behind my son and my son's sons
and so on for generations without end.
Since mountains cannot grow . . .
why shouldn't we be able to level them?"

To this, the wise man had nothing to say.
So the Old Man hoisted his pole and went on his way.

Was he wise? Or was he foolish?

Retold from "How the Fool Moved Mountains" in
Yue Yin Shin (Selected Fables) (Beijing: New World
Publishing, 2002), pp. 9–10. This tale includes Motifs
U260 *Passage of time;* U243 *Courage conquers all and
impossible is made possible;* W20 *Other favorable traits of
character;* and W25 *Equanimity.* One li (as referred to
in the first line) is the equivalent of .621 miles.

One Word for Happiness
A Chinese Folktale

 1 minute, 45 seconds

Chang Kung was head of a large household.
In his compound lived his children, grandchildren, and great-grandchildren, plus assorted aunts, uncles, and cousins.

This family lived together without quarrelling or unpleasantness of any sort.
Everyone got along perfectly.
Even the dogs in Chang Kung's compound did not fight.
Everyone was content and happy all the time.

People talked about this amazing household.
Even the emperor heard of Chang Kung's happy home.
He decided to visit this renowned family.
The emperor was curious: What could be the secret of such happiness?

Chang Kung welcomed the emperor into his home.
The emperor saw that everyone truly seemed mild and happy here.
"Chang Kung, how can all of these persons lives together in such happiness?
What is your secret?"

Chang Kung did not respond.
He simply took out his brush and began to write.
Over and over ... word after word ... he filled the sheet.

Just one word appeared there.
It was written over and over, one hundred times.

The one word was KINDNESS.

"I see," said the emperor.

And taking the brush, the emperor also wrote.
He wrote a proclamation expressing his joy at finding a household
such as that of Chang Kung.
Chang Kung was told to paste this proclamation on his gate,
so that everyone could see the emperor's words.

From that time, Chang Kung's fame grew.
People began to stop by to ask for his picture to paste in their own homes.
They wanted peace and happiness in their homes just as he had created
in his.

To this day Chang Kung's picture hangs in many Chinese kitchens.
He is known as the Kitchen God.
And he reminds everyone of the secret to happiness:
Just one word ... KINDNESS.

Retold from "The God that Lived in the Kitchen" in
Tales of a Chinese Grandmother by Frances Carpenter
(Garden City, New York: Doubleday, 1937), pp. 39–46;
and "God of the Kitchen" in *Tales from Old China* by
Isabelle Chang (New York: Random House, 1948),
pp. 7–9. Motif A411.2. *Kitchen-gods.* Thompson cites
Chinese and Indian variants. MacDonald cites three
Chinese versions of this story.

Medicine to Revive the Dead

A Thai Folktale

1 minute, 20 seconds

It was while the Lord Buddha was staying at Chetawan Garden
that Lady Kisa Khotami's only baby died.

The Lady Kisa was inconsolable.
There must be some way to revive her child.

Clutching the baby in her arms,
she carried the little body to Chetawan Garden.
Pushing through the crowd of people listening to the Buddha's sermon,
she approached the Lord Buddha.

"Dear Lord Buddha, please revive my baby.
Bring him back to life."

The Lord Buddha looked on Kisa with eyes full of pity.

"If you can find me some mustard seeds from a household where death
has not come,
I will make a medicine to revive your child."

Lady Kisa ran from the garden full of hope.
She began to go from door to door in search of these mustard seeds.

"I am looking for a household where nobody has died."

But at each door it was the same answer.

"My grandfather . . . .just died last month."

"My son . . . .died two years ago."
"My mother . . . ."

Lady Kisa went from house to house throughout the entire village.
There was no household that had not been visited by death.

Sadly, she returned to the Lord Buddha.

"Kisa, this is the truth of life," explained the Buddha.
"All who are born must die.
And each household must find a way to live with their own grief."

Now the sad Lady Kisa's mind began to come to rest.
She agreed to let her baby son's body be cremated.

It was this same Lady Kisa who later became
one of the Lord Buddha's most faithful followers.

Retold from "Medicine to Revive the Dead" in *Thai
Tales: Folktales of Thailand* by Supaporn Vathanaprida,
edited by Margaret Read MacDonald (Englewood,
Colorado: Libraries Unlimited, 1994), pp. 64-66. See
that source for a somewhat more lengthy but lovely
source that can be read aloud. MacDonald N135.3.2★
*Cure for all troubles: burn a mustard seed from house which
has no troubles.* MacDonald cites one Cambodian variant. A version in which this story is framed as a riddle
tale appears in *Still More Stories to Solve* by George
Shannon (New York: Greenwillow, 1994), pp. 49-60.

Keeping a Promise
A Chinese Folktale

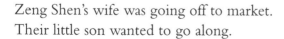

■ 45 seconds

Zeng Shen's wife was going off to market.
Their little son wanted to go along.

"Please, Mother!
I want to go to market with you!
Pleaase . . . "

He kept pleading and following her down the road.

"Go back home," she insisted.
Then, to get him to go home, she told him,
"When I come back we'll kill the pig for you."

That excited the little boy.
So he turned and obediently went back home.

In the evening when the mother returned from the market,
she saw Zeng Shen preparing to kill the pig.

"No! No!" she stopped him.
"I was just saying that to get our son to go home.
I didn't *really* mean that we would kill the pig."

"But we must kill the pig," said Zeng Zhen.
How can you raise a child properly if you deceive him?
Children form their behavior by copying their parents.
Did you want to raise our son to be a liar?"

And so he killed the pig.

Retold from "Why Zeng Shen Killed the Pig" in *Yue Yin Shin
(Selected Fables)* (Beijing: New World Publishing, 2002), p. 36.

Bad Luck or Good Luck?

A Chinese Fable

 1 minute

A young man who was very fond of his fine mare
discovered one day that his horse had run away.

The lad was distraught. "What horrible luck!"

But his father said simply, "Maybe. Maybe not."

A few months later the man's horse returned.
It came galloping up with a handsome stallion by its side!

"What good luck!" cried the young man!

But his father said only, "Maybe. Maybe not."

The young man rode the fine new stallion everywhere.
He was so proud of the horse that he liked to show off on it.
One day he fell from the horse and broke his leg.

"What bad luck!" complained the young man.

Still his father said only, "Maybe. Maybe not."

The very next week a war broke out.
Every able-bodied young man was called to the front to fight.
Most of them were killed.

But the young man with the broken leg was unable to go to battle. And thus he survived.

"You see," said his father. "You never can tell about luck."

A version appears in *Stories of the Spirit, Stories of the Heart: Parables of the Spiritual Path from Around the World*, edited by Christina Feldman and Jack Kornfield (San Francisco: HarperSanFrancisco, 1991), pp. 262-263. This is cited as a Taoist tale and set in northern China. Heather Forest also includes a version of this story in her *Wisdom Tales from Around the World* (August House, 1996), pp. 35-36. MacDonald/Sturm N650.4★ *Two lives saved by luck. Akbar loses a fingertip and Birbal says, "Whatever happens, happens for the best." Banished from the palace. Akbar captured by tribal men and to be sacrificed, let go when realize he is incomplete (no fingertip). Birbal also is saved because had he not been banished he would have been with the king and he would have been sacrificed. India.* MacDonald/Sturm cite this tale as Z51.5★ *Farmer's horse ran off.* See also "That's Good! No, That's Bad!" on page 49 of this collection.

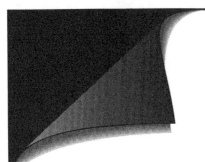

Opening Your Ears
A Speaker's Anecdote

50 seconds

Two men were walking down a city street one day talking.
Suddenly one of the men stopped.

"Listen! A cricket!"

Both men stood still and perked up their ears.

Sure enough a tiny cricket was singing away.
It was hidden under a plant at the sidewalk's edge.

"How did you hear that?" asked the friend.
"Such a tiny sound. I never would have noticed."

"Most folks don't listen for the music of a cricket.
They have their hearts set on something else," said the man who had heard the cricket.

The man stood up and took a penny out of his pocket.
Just as a group of men passed by, he tossed the penny onto the sidewalk.
It hit with a tiny "ping" . . . and every man turned to look.

"See? It all depends on what you are listening for."

This is a favorite story of speakers in the U.S. A telling
by Rona Leventhal is found in *Spinning Tales, Weaving
Hope* edited by Ed Brody, Jay Goldspinner, Katie Gree,
Rona Leventhal, and John Porcino (Philadelphia: New
Society Publishers, 1992), p. 201. Elisa Davy Pearmain
retells it in *Doorways to the Soul* (Cleveland: Pilgrim
Press, 1998), pp. 14–15.

The Miser

A Fable from Aesop

■ 45 seconds

A miser took all of his savings and bought a large lump of gold.
He buried this in a hole in his back yard.
Every day he would come out and check on his gold to make sure it
was still there.

He had no need to spend the gold.
But it made him feel rich to go and look at it.

One day some men were doing work at his neighbor's house.
They noticed that the man came out every day and checked on a certain
spot in his yard.
They became suspicious of his actions.

"He must have something buried there that he is checking on."

So one night they went into his yard and dug around.
They found the gold and made off with it.

When the miser found the empty hole he wept and cried.

He went around feeling miserable for days.

But his friend told him, "Don't grieve like this.
Just take a large stone and put it in the hole and cover it back up.
Pretend that is your gold.
You didn't use it when you had it anyway.
What would the difference be?"

Retold from "The Miser" in *Aesop Without Morals*
by Lloyd W. Daly (New York: Thomas Yoselof, 1961),
p. 187. This might be a good story to tell stock market
investors in times of sinking values.

The Wisdom of the Ants
A Fable from China

▎ 50 seconds

A thousand ants lived on the mountaintop.
Their lives were pleasant enough.
But one day smoke began to creep into their homes.
The ants hurried to see what was wrong.
There below them was a forest fire.
It was coming right up the mountain toward the ants.
It was clear they would all be burnt to death.
The only way to escape was to get beyond the fire.

The ants did not hesitate.
Quickly the one thousand ants formed themselves into a huge ball.
Then they started rolling down the hill.
Right toward the fire!
Faster and faster the ant ball rolled.
Right into the fire!
Right through the fire!
Right beyond the fire!

Then the ball disassembled.
Many, many ants were dead.
Those on the outside of the ball were burnt to death.
They had sacrificed themselves.
But inside the ant ball . . .
many ants still lived.

This was the wisdom of the ants.

Retold from a telling by Chai Ling, one of the
Tiananmen Square survivors in the video *Moving
the Mountain* (Los Angeles: Hallmark Home
Entertainment, 1995).

Very Tiny Tales! Under 30 seconds!

I recently was working with a group of animation students who had been assigned the task of telling a story in animation in just seventeen seconds. This seemed to be almost impossible. The students, for the most part, were not succeeding in getting a story across in that brief time. But when I mentioned this to my storyteller friend Meg Lippert, Meg told me, "Oh I just heard Naomi Baltuck's little daughter, Bea, tell a fifteen-second story." I did not think this could be true. So Meg told me the story and I timed her. Fifteen seconds exactly! And it was a good story, too. Bea's story is below, along with some other very brief tales.

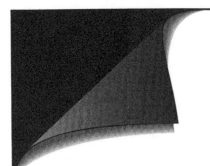

The Man Who Ate Fish

An Iroquois Story
As told by Beatrice Garrard

■ 15 seconds

Once there was a man who ate just one thing,
and that one thing was fish.
One day he ate so much fish,
he turned into one!

Bea's mother, Naomi Baltuck, tells us that Bea read this
story in a display on Iroquois culture at the Iroquois
Museum in upstate New York when she was six and
started telling the story right away. She tells the story
with great intensity. And it works!

The Red Brick Temple

A Thai Tale
As told by Satis Indrakhamheng

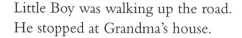 20 seconds

Little Boy was walking up the road.
He stopped at Grandma's house.

"How long will it take me to get to the red brick temple?"
"I don't know," said Grandma.

Little Boy started walking on up the road.

"It will take you two hours," called Grandma.
"But a minute ago you said you didn't know," said Little Boy.

"I had to see how fast you were walking."

Told to Margaret Read MacDonald in English
August 10, 2001 by Satis Indrakhamheng, a physician
from Bangkok visiting Guemes Island in Washington
State. This little jest is told widely in the U.S. these
days. Usually the walker is a man in a country setting.
The farmer responds dryly and then calls out after the
walker as he moves on down the road.

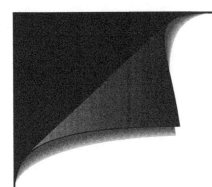

The Thai Man in the Shade

A Contemporary Fable from Thailand
As told by Supaporn Vathanaprida

■ 30 seconds

An American saw a Thai man sitting in the shade of a tree.
The Thai man was just sitting there, doing nothing.
The American asked, "Dear friend, how can you sit here doing nothing?
Why don't you work?"

"Why should I work?" asked the Thai.

"Well, if you work hard you will earn a lot of money.
If you work for many years, one day you will be rich.
Then you will be free to do anything you want.
You could travel, go where you want,
Or just sit and do nothing."

The Thai looked at the American incredulously.
"But that is what I am doing now.
Just sitting here, doing nothing."

From *Thai Tales: Folktales of Thailand* by Supaporn
Vathanaprida. edited by Margaret Read MacDonald
(Englewood, Colorado: Libraries Unlimited), p. 121.
A similar tale is recounted in *Stories of the Spirit, Stories
of the Heart: Parables of the Spiritual Path from Around
the World*, edited by Christina Feldman and Jack
Kornfield (San Francisco: HarperSanFrancisco, 1991),
pp. 306–307. They set the story in the U.S. and show a
rich industrialist from the north speaking to a southern fisherman.

Holding up the Sky
A Fable from China

■ 30 seconds

One day an elephant saw a hummingbird lying
flat on its back on the ground.
The bird's tiny feet were raised up into the air.

"What on earth are you doing, Hummingbird?"
asked the elephant.

The hummingbird replied.
"I have heard that the sky might fall today.
If that should happen,
I am ready to do my bit in holding it up."

The elephant laughed and mocked the tiny bird.

"Do you think *those* little feet could hold up the sky?"

"Not alone," admitted the hummingbird.
"But each must do what he can.
And this is what *I* can do."

Retold from "Holding up the Sky" in *Peace Tales:
World Folktales to Talk About* by Margaret Read
MacDonald (North Haven, Connecticut: Linnet
Books, 1992), p. 99. Another version may be found in
Tales from Old China by Isabelle Chang (New York:
Random House, 1948) pp. 9–10. Motif B300 *Helpful
animal.* MacDonald/Sturm B300.0.1★ *Hummingbird
does his part in holding up sky.* One teller told me that
she had changed the ending; she has elephant lie
down and put his feet up to help. I like that.

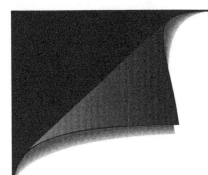

The Bilingual Mouse

A Contemporary Story
As told by Sharon Creeden

■ 30 seconds

One day a mother mouse was out taking her babies for a walk.
A large cat came to frighten them.

"Quick, children, run and hide."

The mousekins ran and hid behind a large rock.
Mother mouse positioned herself between her children and the cat.
When the cat drew near, the mother mouse said,

BOW WOW!
BOW WOW!

The frightened and confused cat ran away.

All the mousekins came running to their mother.
She told them, "Observe, children, the benefits of learning a second language."

Seattle storyteller Sharon Creeden heard this story
from Bob Barton of Toronto. Bob told her he heard
it from another Toronto teller, Alice Kane. For a much
longer rendition hear Antonio Sacre's CD, *The Barking
Mouse and Other Tales of Wonder: Stories by Antonio Sacre*
(Chicago: Woodside Avenue Music Productions,
2000). His version is also featured in a picture book,
The Barking Mouse by Antonio Sacre and illustrated
by Alfredo Aguirre (Morton Grove, Illinois: Albert
Whitman, 2003).

The Bilingual Cat
A Mexican-American Folktale

■ 35 seconds

Once upon a time, a cat was chasing a mouse.
The mouse ran into a hole.
"I'm safe," he said.
But outside he could hear,
"Meow! Meow!"

"I'd better stay safe inside," he thought.

The meowing stopped.
He waited.
He peeked outside.
He could see the cat's whiskers.

"I'd better stay safe inside."

Suddenly he heard, *BOW WOW! BOW WOW!*

The mouse said, "Oh! A dog must have chased away that big, bad cat.
It's safe to go outside."
He left the hole.

The cat caught him and ate him.
And after she cleaned her whiskers, she settled down for a nap.
Just before she fell asleep, she said,
"*Bow wow!* It pays to be bilingual."

As retold by Seattle teller Sharon Creeden. The story
appears in *Mexican-American Folklore* by John O. West
(Little Rock: August House, 1988), p. 92.

Endless Tales
and Tales
to End
the Telling

These short story-enders can be told very briefly or can be stretched if you want to pull the audience's leg a bit longer. They act as a humorous excuse to stop the storytelling session.

Mother Morey

A Story from the U.S.

■ 10 seconds

I'll tell you a story of Mother Morey.
And now our story's begun.

I'll tell you another
about her brother.
And now our story is done.

Told to me by Jane Lopez-Santillana. Jane's mother
told her children this story when they were little. It
annoyed them greatly, says Jane.

The Rats of Nagasaki

A Folktale from Japan

▌ 1 minute or longer, depending on how
long you tease your audience

It was a hard time in the city of Nagasaki.
Food was scarce.
Even the rats had nothing to eat.
So the rats decided to sail over to Satsuma and find food there.

When they were out on the sea,
They saw another ship approaching.
It was a ship from Satsuma,
and crowding the railings were rats!

"Nagasaki rats!" called the Satsuma rats.
"We are sailing to Nagasaki to find food.
There is nothing at all to eat in Satsuma."

"But we are sailing to Satsuma to find food!"
called the Nagasaki rats.
"There is nothing at all to eat in Nagasaki!"

"Oh, despair." One of the Nagasaki rats jumped overboard.

"Oh, despair." One of the Satsuma rats jumped overboard.

"Oh, despair." Another of the Nagasaki rats jumped overboard.

"Oh, despair." Another of the Satsuma rats jumped overboard.

▌ Keep this up until someone calls a stop.

Well, since the rats are all hopeless . . .
this tale is too.
We'd better give it up right here.

Retold from "The Rats of Nagasaki" in Carl Withers,
I Saw a Rocket Walk a Mile (New York: Holt, 1965),
p. 129. Motif Z11 *Endless Tales.* MacDonald Z11.3★
Endless tale. Rats of Nagasaki meet rats of Satsuma.

The Tinkling Bell

A Folktale from Japan

1 minute or longer, depending on how
long you tease your audience

There was once a monastery that had a tiny bell.
When the wind blew, the bell made such a sweet, tinkling sound.
The monk who lived there loved the sound of that bell.

One day a man from the village asked if he could borrow the bell.
Well, what could the monk say?
Of course the man could borrow the bell.

One week passed . . .
Two weeks . . .
The monk really missed the tinkling of that bell.

So he sent a servant to bring it back.
But when he reached the home of that man,
there was the man . . . ringing the little bell and dancing.
The servant heard that tinkling sound and . . .
he began to dance too!

Since the servant did not come back,
The monk sent another servant to fetch him.
But when *that* servant heard the bell . . .
he began to dance too!

So he sent *another* servant to find out what was happening.
And when he heard the bell . . .
He began to dance too!
So . . .

■ Continue until someone asks when you are going to stop.

Well, we can't continue until they all come back.
I guess we could send someone to find out how the story ends . . .
but they would probably just start dancing too!

Retold from Miroslav Novak, *Fairy Tales from Japan*
(New York: Hamlyn, 1970), pp. 31–36. Motif Z11
Endless tales. MacDonald Z11.6★ *Endless tale: monk has
tiny bell, he is content hearing it tinkle. Apothecary borrows
and does not return. Servant sent for bell finds A. dancing
and cannot resist joining him. Etc. If we send someone to
find out how story ends, they'll stay too.* MacDonald cites
one Japanese variant. Sheila Dailey has a nice
retelling of this motif in her *Putting the World in a
Nutshell* (New York: H. W. Wilson, 1994), pp. 65-66.
See also Motif D1415 *Magic object causes person to
dance.* Thompson cites variants from England, Wales,
Iceland, the U.S., Italy, the Gold Coast, India, and
Breton. MacDonald cites variants from Denmark,
Yugoslavia, Spain, Portugal, Algeria, Russia, Latvia,
Ireland, Norway, Germany, Luxembourg, Korea, the
Congo, and Uganda. MacDonald and Sturm include
sources from Sierra Leone, Brazil, Ireland, Jamaica,
Cajun, Germany, and South Africa. In these tales the
motif appears as part of a longer tale.

The Shepherd and His Sheep

A Folktale from Czechoslovakia

■ 1 minute, 15 seconds or longer, depending
on how long you tease your audience

A shepherd with a large flock of sheep took them out to pasture every day.
To reach the pasture they had to wade across a little brook.
One day it was already late when the shepherd started for home.
The sun was setting, and he was in a great hurry to reach home.
But when he came to the brook,
he saw that rains had swollen the stream until it was too deep to wade across.
The only thing he could do was to take his sheep downstream to the foot-
bridge and drive them across there.
But that footbridge was so narrow . . .
Only one sheep could cross at a time.
The shepherd drove the first sheep across the bridge.
Then he drove the second sheep across the bridge.
Then he drove the third sheep across.
He drove the fourth sheep across.
The fifth sheep . . .
The sixth sheep . . .

We'll have to wait until he gets the sheep all across the bridge.

■ Teller stops and waits. When the audience asks him to continue, he says . . .

"Oh, no!
It took the sheep so long to cross the bridge
that it is now morning already.
The shepherd has to drive the sheep back to pasture.

He drove the first sheep across the footbridge.

Then he drove the second sheep across the bridge.
Then he drove the third sheep across.
He drove the fourth sheep across.
The fifth sheep . . .
The sixth sheep . . .

Retold from "The Story That Never Ends" in Parker
Fillmore, *Czechoslovak Fairy Tales* (New York:
Harcourt, Brace, 1919), p. 243. Motif Z11 *Endless
tales. Hundreds of sheep to be carried over stream one at a
time, etc. The wording of the tale so arranged as to continue
indefinitely.* Thompson cites sources from Spain, India,
Ireland, Italy, and Germany. Tale Type 2300 *Endless
Tales. Hundreds of sheep to be carried over stream one at a
time, endless quacking of geese, etc.* Aarne-Thompson cite
sources from Lithuania, Iceland, Scotland, Ireland,
England, France, Spain, the Netherlands, Italy,
Hungary, Russia, India, China, Puerto Rico, Brazil,
the U.S., and others.

The Golden Key

A German Folktale

1 minute, 15 seconds or longer, depending
on how long you tease your audience

One cold winter day, a boy took his sledge to the forest for wood. He had
to work for quite a while at this, so he decided to make a little fire to
warm himself up. First he had to clear away the snow so that he could
build a fire on the ground.

As he scooped away the snow . . . suddenly something caught his eye.
It was a little golden key!

"How strange! But if there is a key, there must be a lock." And the boy
began to dig about in the snow, searching. He looked this way . . . and that
way . . . and . . . here was what he was looking for! A trunk! "I'll bet the key
fits this lock!"

The boy bent down and tried to fit the key into the lock. No.
It wouldn't fit.

He tried again. No.

"But it *must* fit!" said the boy. "Why would there be a key if it wouldn't
unlock the trunk?"

So he bent over again. And this time, very carefully, he eased the key into
the lock. Yes! It did fit! Perfectly!

The boy was so excited! Aren't you excited too? Whatever could be inside
that trunk buried under snow so deep in the forest?

The boy turned the key . . .

He turned the key again. . . .

Oh, well. It might take him some time to get that trunk open.

We will just have to wait until he has unlocked the trunk and lifted the lid before we find out what is inside.

Retold from "The Golden Key" in *Tales of Laughter* by Kate Douglas Wiggin and Nora Archibald Smith (New York: McClure Company, 1908), p. 82. This is Grimms' folktale No. 200 "The Golden Key." Motif Z12 *Unfinished tales.* Under Z12.2* *Boy finds box, key, what's inside,* MacDonald cites Wanda Gág, *More Tales From Grimm* (New York: Coward-McCann, 1947, x), and a Jewish Russian variant in Mira Ginsburg, *Three Rolls and a Doughnut: Fables from Russia* (New York: Dial, 1970), p. 27. A nice retelling is included in Sheila Dailey's *Putting the World in a Nutshell* (New York: H.W. Wilson, 1994), p. 73. Or see any complete Grimms collection for the tale.

MORE SHORT TALES FOR TELLING

Each of these collections contains several brief stories along with longer pieces. Some, such as George Shannon's riddling collections, are *all* quick tells!

TALES TO MAKE YOU THINK

Daly, Lloyd W. *Aesop Without Morals*. New York: Thomas Yoseloff, 1961.

Feldman, Christina, and Jack Kornfield, eds. *Stories of the Spirit, Stories of the Heart: Parables of the Spiritual Path from Around the World*. San Francisco: HarperSanFrancisco, 1991.

Forest, Heather. *Wisdom Tales from Around the World*. Little Rock: August House, 1996.

MacDonald, Margaret Read. *Earth Care: World Folktales to Talk About*. North Haven, Connecticut: Linnet Books, 1999.

MacDonald, Margaret Read. *Peace Tales: World Folktales to Talk About*. North Haven, Connecticut: Linnet Books, 1992.

Pearmain, Elisa Davy. *Doorways to the Soul: 52 Wisdom Tales from Around the World*. Cleveland: Pilgrim Press, 1998.

White, William P. *Stories for Telling: A Treasury for Christian Storytellers*. Minneapolis: Augsburg, 1986.

RIDDLING TALES

Jaffe, Nina, and Steve Zeitlin. *The Cow of No Color: Riddle Stories and Justice Tales from Around the World*. New York: Holt, 1998.

Shannon, George, and John O'Brien, illus. *More True Lies: Eighteen Tales for You to Judge*. New York: Greenwillow, 2001.

Shannon, George, and John O'Brien, illus. *True Lies: Eighteen Tales for You to Judge*. New York: Greenwillow, 1997.

Shannon, George, and Peter Sís, illus. *More Stories to Solve: Fifteen Folktales from Around the World*. New York: Greenwillow, 1990.

Shannon, George, and Peter Sís, illus. *Still More Stories to Solve: Fourteen Folktales from Around the World*. New York: Greenwillow, 1994.

Shannon, George, and Peter Sís, illus. *Stories to Solve: Folktales from Around the World*. New York: HarperCollins, 1985.

STORYTIME STRETCHES AND CAMP LORE

Baltuck, Naomi, and Doug Cushman, illus. *Crazy Gibberish and Other Story Hour Stretches (from a storyteller's bag of tricks)*. Hamden, Connecticut: Linnet Books, 1993.

Carlson, Bernice Wells. *Listen! And Help Tell the Story*. Nashville: Abingdon, 1965.

Tashjian, Virginia. *Juba This and Juba That*. Boston: Little, Brown, 1969.

Tashjian, Virginia. *With a Deep Sea Smile*. Boston: Little, Brown, 1969.

ACTION RHYMES

Cobb, Jane. *I'm a Little Teapot! Presenting Preschool Storytime*. Vancouver: Black Sheep Press, 1996.

Defty, Jeff. *Creative Fingerplays & Action Rhymes: An Index and Guide to Their Use*. Phoenix: Oryx Press, 1992.

SHORT FOLKTALES

Dailey, Sheila. *Putting the World in a Nutshell: The Art of the Formula Tale*. New York: H.W. Wilson, 1994.

Hardendorff, Jeanne B. *Just One More*. Philadelphia: J.B. Lippincott, 1969.

Webster, M.L. *On the Trail Made of Dawn: Native American Creation Stories*. North Haven, Connecticut: Linnet Books, 2001.

STORIES INCORPORATING STRING FIGURES, PAPER-FOLDING, AND OTHER OBJECTS

Fujita, Hiroko, and Fran Stallings, ed. *Stories to Play With: Kids' Tales Told with Puppets, Paper, Toys, and Imagination*. Little Rock: August House, 1999.

Pellowski, Anne. *The Family Storytelling Handbook: How to Use Stories, Anecdotes, Rhymes, Handkerchiefs, Paper and Other Objects to Enrich Your Family Traditions*. New York: Macmillan, 1987.

Pellowski, Anne. *Hidden Stories in Plants: Unusual and Easy-to-Tell Stories from Around the World, Together with Creative Things to Do While Telling Them*. New York: Macmillan, 1990.

Pellowski, Anne. *The Story Vine: A Source Book of Unusual and Easy-to Tell Stories from Around the World*. New York: Macmillan, 1984.

Pellowski, Anne. *The Storyteller's Handbook: A Young People's Collection of Unusual Tales and Helpful Hints on How to Tell Them*. New York: Simon and Schuster, 1995.

SCARY TALES

MacDonald, Margaret Read. *When the Lights Go Out: Twenty Scary Tales to Tell*. New York: H.W. Wilson, 1988.

Schwartz, Alvin. *More Scary Stories to Tell in the Dark*. New York: HarperCollins, 1980.

Schwartz, Alvin. *Scary Stories 3: More Tales to Chill Your Bones*. New York: HarperCollins, 1991.

Schwartz, Alvin. *Stories to Tell in the Dark*. New York: Lippincott, 1981.